The Life of Doshie

The Life of Doshie

One Man's Journey through Life

CLAUDE B. MCQUEEN SR.

Sharecropper, Farm Life, Husband, Father, Vietnam Vet,
Grandfather, Great-Grandfather ...
All Lead to the Life I Love

Doshie 1953 age 8

iUniverse, Inc.
Bloomington

The Life of Doshie
One Man's Journey through Life

iUniverse books may be ordered through booksellers or by contacting:

iUniverse
1663 Liberty Drive
Bloomington, IN 47403
www.iuniverse.com
1-800-Authors (1-800-288-4677)

Because of the dynamic nature of the Internet, any web addresses or links contained in this book may have changed since publication and may no longer be valid. The views expressed in this work are solely those of the author and do not necessarily reflect the views of the publisher, and the publisher hereby disclaims any responsibility for them.

Any people depicted in stock imagery provided by Thinkstock are models, and such images are being used for illustrative purposes only.

Certain stock imagery © Thinkstock.

ISBN: 978-1-4620-1166-7 (sc)
ISBN: 978-1-4620-1165-0 (hc)
ISBN: 978-1-4620-1164-3 (e)

Library of Congress Control Number: 2011907617

Printed in the United States of America

iUniverse rev. date: 07/08/2011

This book was written for my children, grandchildren, great-grandchildren, and great-great-grandchildren.

In loving memory of Mary A. McQueen, Caroline D. McQueen, Caroline McQueen, Willie Wilkerson, Johnnie McQueen, Robert Wilkerson, Bob Byrd, Ella Purifoy, Mary B. Purifoy, Wallace Vaughan, and Betty Mc Laughlin. Rachael Purifoy McQueen died before completion of this book Thank you to my family and friends.

Acknowledgments

Special thanks to Erik and Crystal Talford. Without their input, this book could not have been put together so nicely.

Thanks to Cindy Calderon for her introduction to iUniverse.

Thanks to Burl and Mary Purifoy.

Thanks to all who helped with my struggle through tough times.

Thank you to my wife Marie McQueen who supported me from the beginning. Without her help and assistance this would not have been possible!

My Grandparents

Grandfather
Tyler McQueen   married   Grandmother
                                                            Tillie Dockery

Their Children

1. Eva McQueen Blue   my aunt
2. Lucy McQueen McNeil   my aunt
3. Florence McQueen (never married)   my aunt
4. Anna Bell McQueen McLeod   my aunt
5. Elnora McQueen (never married)   my aunt
6. Caroline McQueen Wilkerson   my mother
7. Dempsey McQueen (never married)   my uncle
8. Jurdee Lee McQueen   my uncle
9. Claude McQueen (never married)   my uncle

My Parents

Father
Willie McLean

Mother
Caroline McQueen Wilkerson

My Siblings

1. Robert L. Wilkerson   my brother
2. Willie F. Wilkerson   my brother
3. Lois Jean Wilkerson (died as an infant)   my sister
4. Daisy Mae McQueen Byrd   my sister
5. Curtiss McLaughlin   my brother
6. Lester W. McQueen   my brother
7. Johnnie B. McQueen   my brother

I never knew my grandparents; they died before I was born. I was named after my uncle Claude—he also died before I was born. All my aunts and uncles looked like Native Americans. My mother told me they all were part Cherokee. Aunt Florence worked as a domestic house servant in High Point, North Carolina, for many years and would visit us when she could. Aunt Lucy was born in Wagram, North Carolina, and stayed there all her life, raising a nice, large family. Her married name was McNeil. Aunt Eva married Nero Blue and together, they worked a farm in North Carolina before moving to Freeport, Long Island, New York. Aunt Anna Bell lived all her life in North Carolina, and I remember her for being a great cook. Aunt Elnora was loved, and she gave love. She was so very sweet and had long wavy hair. She would prepare lunch or sandwiches for me when I visited her, and she always had time for me. I remember that she puzzled me because she chose to drink ice water in the winter—I thought ice water was a drink for the hot summer months. Aunt Elnora always talked *to* me, not down to me. I always felt good around her.

Sometimes when Mommy and I would spend the night at Aunt Elnora's house, she would let me listen to country songs on the radio from Nashville, Tennessee, home of the Grand Ole Opry. I never knew why she never married. I guess she chose to stay single.

None of my aunts or uncles ever yelled at me or beat me for any reason. They all told me to stay out of trouble, to never steal even one penny, because that could lead me to steal more pennies.

~THE BEGINNINGS~

I was born in 1945 into a world where color televisions were unheard of, and all cars were the same color—black. Cars were started by cranking them with an iron bar at the front. Cars didn't have air conditioning, power brakes, or automatic transmission—all cars were standard shift. Black men wore their hair in a crew cut or marcel. There were no such things as cell phones, DVDs, CDs, boom boxes, iPods, fax, or Internet. If you needed to reach someone fast, you sent a letter via air mail or special delivery—fast contact was three days via air mail.

A funeral wake was just that—the body of the deceased would be brought to his or her home, and family would sit awake with the body until morning; that's why it's called a wake. Doctors did house calls back then, day or night. Most common colds were treated with herbs or roots or what was called catnip tea—these were leaves that grew wild on a bush. (See "Home-Grown Medical Treatments" at the back of this book.)

A coke was five cents. A loaf of bread was seven cents. A haircut for a boy was fifteen cents, unless he was older than thirteen years old; then it was twenty to fifty cents. Most houses had wood-burning fireplaces. Some had heaters that used charcoal. Very few houses had telephones, and those that did had phones that were black with a rotary dial. School clothes were brown khaki pants, a plaid shirt, and penny loafers and checkered socks. Girls wore dresses—no slacks or jeans—with white bobby socks and usually black loafers.

There were no fast-food places—no McDonald's, Burger King, or Wendy's. There were a few mom-and-pop places to buy chips, Coke, and sometimes a chicken sandwich. The popular place to go on a date was the drive-in movie, where you would drive up in your car to a sound box (about the size of your fist) and watch a movie from your car.

There were no public restrooms available anywhere for colored people; only whites could use the restrooms. That's the way it was from the 1950s until the mid-1960s.

We didn't iron our clothes with an electric iron. To iron clothes, we would place a heavy-duty steel iron near the fireplace, let the face of the iron get hot, and then use it to iron. Most people who could afford two irons would alternate them, using one while the other got hot.

Girls in the 1950s would use an item of clothing called a can-can to make the skirts of their dresses stand in an outspread style. Can-cans were made of wire and fastened around the waist. Girls would use them mostly when they went out dancing. In the 1950s, all dancing spots were known as "juke joints," where you would go on a Friday or Saturday night to have a good time. The jukebox was known as a "pickoloo." After inserting a dime, you could select your favorite singer; a quarter would get three selections.

I was five years old in 1950, and I remember vividly that my mom would pull me on a sack as she picked cotton in the field. Some days the sun was so hot that she would place me under a bush and make me stay in the shade, and she would bring me water from the yard pump. There wasn't ice for drinks in those days. I can recall the day my youngest brother, Johnnie, was born. My sister Daisy brought my brother Lester and me out in the yard to play and said we had to stay outside for a while. Then I saw strange women go into our house (I didn't know that these were the midwives). Shortly after, I remember hearing a baby crying. I could not understand, because I knew there was not a baby in the house when I'd gone outside. The next day, my mother told me I had a baby brother and let me see him.

I started school at age seven—that was the age when children entered first grade in those days. I heard the walk to school was a mile, and of course, it was another mile back home. But I wanted to be in first grade; this meant I was a big boy. When that day came in August 1952, my older sister, who was eighteen at the time and no longer in school herself, brought me to school and waited under a shade tree until school was out to bring me home. My teacher's name was Mrs. Sparks. (Mrs. Sparks was still alive in 2008, living in a nursing home in Fayetteville, North Carolina. My older brother Curtiss told me that she said she remembered me as "Doshie.")

School was inside a big one-room clapboard barn. This room held first through fourth grades. There were only four or five students in each grade. As you passed to the next grade, you moved around the room. Once a month the principal came from nearby Shaw High School to see how the students were doing during class. I must have been a good student because Mrs. Sparks asked my mother if she could take me home on some Fridays and bring me back for school on Monday.

Mrs. Sparks and her husband had no children of their own; I assumed I was company for them. They were lonesome in their big red-brick house by themselves. Their house was just the opposite from ours. They had lights, hot water, and inside heat. We had no lights, no inside plumbing, and no inside heat. But we were happy.

I say I lived in a "condo," even before condominiums were built, because we had what I referred to as upper and lower living. Our house had a large attic above our living space, and we often climbed up there—our "upper" living. And our kitchen was about twenty-five feet out from the main house (our "lower" living) and had big ceiling-to-floor windows. The windows were covered by wooden slats that swung outward to allow sunshine into the house, but there were no glass panes in these windows.

We used two long wooden benches as chairs. We had tin pans for plates and tin cups to drink water. When we had sugar in the house, which was not often, we would have pure sugar water. The staple foods were Grandma's Molasses (a popular brand), fat-back meat, and white bread. The best meal would come on Sunday after church, when Mommy would tell us which chicken to catch from our flock. Then she would either wring or chop the head off and then pluck it, and boil or fry it for us to have with dried field peas and sometimes rice. We could only get one piece of chicken. Sometimes I would be so, so hungry, I could not wait for dinner, and if Mommy was not looking, I would try to steal a piece of chicken out of the hot grease. I did not know that Mommy could tell right away when I did it.

Our stove and fireplace used wood. It was a big job for us boys to go into the woods each day to gather enough firewood to keep warm. Mommy would come along with us, and I felt bad, seeing her tote wood on her back. It hurt me, but I was too young to know how to do everything. I did not know it then, but she was teaching me how to fend for myself.

Our house was poorly constructed. The clapboard on the side of the house was paper thin, and the roof consisted of very thin sheets of tin. The tin roof had small holes in it, so when I was in bed at night, I could look up and see the stars in the sky. When it rained, the water would drip through those holes, so we had to keep moving our bed from spot to spot. Our house and others like it were originally built for slaves, but later on, they were used for the people who helped the sharecropper work the fields. The owner of the plantation was very selective about who lived in his houses. If there was a family with a man and mostly sons, that family would get the stronger house, because they could provide more help or manpower to the land owner. We had no man in our house. Dad was never around, and I missed that part of my life so very much. My mother and all of her children who lived in the house were expected to work for the sharecropper. In this way, we helped to pay the rent for living in his house and on his land. At the end of the harvest, we would receive a little cash payout for our work, but it was never more than forty to sixty dollars for the year.

I can remember Mommy getting up early to make a fire in the fireplace to try to get the room warm enough for us to get up for school. We boys would stand near the fireplace, trying to dry off because we were so wet from bed-wetting, but we would still end up stinking in school because we had no inside bathroom to wash our bodies. We would not be the only ones; half the class seemed to have had the same problem.

In those days, we went to school to learn, Monday through Friday, and that's what we did. We also had recess for fifteen minutes each day to play in the yard. We played hopscotch, jump rope, tag, wrestling, boxing, and horseshoe games. We had fun—good fun.

For lunch, if we had thirteen cents, we could have a hot meal and milk at Wagram School. No soda was sold. Many days, all my mother could give us was a piece of corn bread and fat-back meat. There were very few times that she could afford the three cents for milk, and when she couldn't, we drank water. On Saturdays we would stay around the house. We had no television or radio for years in our house. We made our own entertainment, playing with old car tires and climbing trees—this was country life.

On Sunday, Mommy would get us ready for church. We had to walk a mile to church—it was next door to my school. It was a Baptist church. On our way to church, sometimes the preacher and his wife would pass us by in their car, but they never stopped to ask if we wanted a ride, even though their car was empty. I was very ashamed that he treated us that way, he being a man of God.

In church, the preacher would get the members in a frenzy. The women would shout all over the place and fall down, foaming at the mouth, while others fanned them. After church, the return trip home would be the same—no one would ask if we wanted a ride. So we walked. Some summer days it would be so hot that we could not walk on the highway because the asphalt was melting, and we could have been burned very badly.

After church, we all looked forward to a chicken dinner. Mommy would point to the chicken that was to be our dinner for the day. We boys all had a number of chicks we called our own, and I was always sad when Mommy pointed to one of mine. But we had to eat. After the chicken died, Mommy would show us how to dip the chicken in hot water quickly and then pluck off the feathers. Then she showed us how to hold it over an open flame to singe the leftover tiny feathers. The hard part was opening up the chicken and taking out the "bad" part (the gall bladder) while saving the "good" parts (the liver and gizzard). When we removed the liver and gizzard, we had to be very careful not to tear the gall bladder, which is located under the liver of the chicken. If the gall bladder is accidentally cut or torn, it spills a very bitter-tasting liquid over the good parts, and then they can't be eaten.

My mother made the best dumplings. After a bowl of her dumplings and a piece of chicken, I soon forgot about how the chicken started out.

That would be the last of chicken for another week. The chicks in the yard seemed to know it as well. During summer, Mommy always had a small vegetable garden. We also gathered wild berries in the woods, so we made do with what we had, which was very little to nothing.

One Saturday when I was very young, my brother gave me a ride on the rear of a very old bike. My right heel became caught in the back spokes of the bike and cut me very bad. To stop the bleeding, my brother packed the cut with dirt from the ground. At that time there was only one doctor for the whole town. He would make house calls when necessary, but first someone would have to call him and tell him about the medical problem. Then the doctor would say when he could come out to the person's house. If it was a medical emergency, the doctor would call for the town rescue squad to bring that person to the hospital. But we had no phone to call him and no car to drive to his office, so we had to use whatever means we could to find the doctor. My mother asked someone with a mule and wagon to take me about three miles to the doctor. At that time the doctors used clamps, not stitches, for a severe wound. As he clamped my heel, I inadvertently kicked a box of medical supplies off the table, but he didn't get angry. I remember how calm he was about it. With that clamp on my heel, I was unable to walk for a long time. I had to slide around the house and the yard until I started to heal.

Not so long afterward, I had yet another problem. One day I was standing too close to the open fireplace, and my pants caught fire. I was so scared that I ran out of the house. My sister was home, and she knocked me down and beat out the flames. Thanks to my sister Daisy Mae, I didn't burn to death, but my right leg and side were severely damaged. I wasn't burned anywhere else. Again, I could not walk for quite some time. My mother told me it was a year before I could walk again.

Meanwhile, my mother had to double up on the work by helping the owner's wife in her house; this was to make up for my loss in the field. The land owner would come to the house to see how I was healing because he wanted me back in the field. They had no mercy in those days—if you lived on their land, then you worked their land. When I was finally healed, I was happy to be able to walk again. I'd been sliding around for so long and watching my brothers play when I couldn't, and it was good to be back on my feet.

When I was about ten years old, I thought about what I wanted to be when I became a man: I wanted to be a long-distance truck driver. The long eighteen-wheel trucks seemed like they would be fun to drive. We lived along a stretch of a Highway 301 (now I-95), and I would watch these big trucks roll by day and night, heading north and south. Some days, I would stand by the roadside and pump my arm, which was a way to ask the drivers to pull the cord to make the big horns atop the truck blow. This seemed like a top-of-the-world job. I wanted a big white house to live in, with one room filled with candy, floor to ceiling. My favorite candy was Baby Ruth candy bars, Hershey bars, M&M's plain, and Mr. Goodbar. I could only get candy maybe once every month and half, so I said that once I grew up, I would have plenty.

And the big white house? To me, everyone who lived in a white house was rich in everything—good food all the time; the kids seemed to have the best toys; the parents drove the big cars. I knew nothing about the hard work that went into having and maintaining a big white house. Some ten-year-old boys were learning the key things about farming or becoming a good hunter—this is what country life taught. Country life did not teach someone to become a long-distance truck driver, but I wanted to be just that.

My brother Lester eventually became a long-distance truck driver, and I was able to ride the roads with him. He also showed me how to ride the Greyhound bus, and by 1957 I was old enough to ride for the first time by myself. It cost fifteen cents to go from Wagram to Laurinburg. I remember how afraid I was to stand on the side of the road in Wagram, waiting for the bus. Lester never used the bus himself; he would always hitchhike or bum a ride with a stranger. I did not have the nerve to do that.

The first movie I saw by myself was *Fire Down Below* (1959), about a fire on a ship at sea—fifteen cents to see it. It was a good movie, but afterward, I was scared to go back home, because the last bus left the station near dark, and I had to know when to pull the cord so the driver would let me off at the right crossroad that would go by my house. Then

I'd have to battle dogs that would bite me along the mile-and-a-half walk. I always planted a huge stick in the bushes before I got on the bus to go to Laurinburg, because it came in handy to help me get home without a dog biting me. I knew to never let the dog get behind me; the dog would have the upper hand when he was behind me.

I never owned a large dog. My own dogs were always medium-size and were very good house dogs. They would not let anyone walk up to the house. People had to yell or blow their horn before they could come to the door. For a few years, we had no dogs, but we always had cats.

For extra food, my brothers Lester and Johnnie and I would fish in the small creek, and everything we caught would be enjoyed by the whole family. Wild blueberries and huckleberries were plentiful. We also would steal a watermelon from a field from time to time. The melon would always be too heavy to tote, so we would just roll it home down the highway.

I never wore shoes in summer months, but my mother could not afford them anyway. Sometimes, after picking cotton all week from sunup till sundown, we might make four to six dollars among all of us. The owner sometimes paid a dollar per one hundred pounds of cotton, and we had to pick hard and fast to get that amount. Along the way, we had to crawl on our knees and fight all kinds of bugs and spiders. Sometimes green snakes would blend right in with the color of the cotton leaf, and we would not know it was a snake until we'd already picked it up. When that happened to me, my whole body would go numb and cold—that's how bad it would scare me. Also during the summer on the farm, we had to be very careful not to be stung by wasps or yellow jackets. Once we were stung, we remembered it for a long time.

The sun baked all day long. For dinner (what might now be called lunch), people usually ate a honey bun, Pepsi, and a quarter pound of bologna. This was bought on credit from the land owner's store because he owned everything. Some people would walk a mile or more back to their homes to eat dinner. I remember one day when I was eleven years old, I walked home for dinner and decided to fry some corn bread. As I turned the bread over quickly, the hot grease splashed on my stomach. Even today, I have the burn mark to show for it.

Sometimes the owner of the field would pay us on the spot when we finished our day's work, or sometimes he would come at noon on Saturdays. Any time the owner paid us was a joyful moment. When there was money, Mommy would measure our feet with a string and travel by Greyhound bus to Laurinburg, North Carolina—about fifteen miles away—to buy us shoes from the second-hand store. We never knew what we would get; all we knew was that we might get a pair, and we were happy and could not wait for her to return home. My shoes cost twenty-five cents, my brother Lester's cost thirty cents, and my baby brother Johnnie's cost ten cents. If she had any extra money, she would buy some used clothes for us, although they were always too big so that we could grow into them. We were always very pleased with what we got.

When I was about eight years old, I had to have my tonsils removed—they hurt me when I would eat. The welfare service in those days would treat poor people with medical needs without cost. I remember the day I was to go to the hospital. Mommy and I waited all morning for a person to come for us and drive us to the hospital. I did not want to go, but I was tired of hurting all the time. The hospital was Scotland Memorial in Laurinburg, North Carolina.

Before the doctor operated on me, a nurse poured ether on a cloth and told me to smell it. Before I knew it, I was out cold. When I woke up, my mother and brother Willie were by my side. I had a black collar with ice in it around my neck. Mommy had stayed all night with me, sleeping on the floor. I was given Jell-O and ice cream to eat. My throat was very sore.

Years later, Mommy told me that the doctor had wanted to remove my adenoids as well, but she would not allow it because she did not want to put me in any more pain. That is why, even to this day, I snore loudly when sleeping. Often, snoring is caused by adenoids blocking the windpipe.

A year or so after that, in Wagram, North Carolina, I was saddened by something that was about to happen but that I could not stop. I was getting a fifty-cent haircut in a little hut of a barbershop. As I was sitting in the chair, I saw a white dog lie down under the rear wheel of a truck, probably resting from the heat of the day. Then I saw the truck driver get in the truck. I thought the dog surely would hear the truck start up and would move from under the wheel, but he did not, and the truck killed him. I wondered for a long time why I did not jump out of the chair and make the driver aware of the dog. But I was just a boy and didn't know what action to take.

I continued to learn many things as I grew up on the farm. I learned how to plow the field with a mule. And I learned farm words—words that I would only use on the farm. For example, if I wanted a mule to do certain things, I used the words that the mule understood. To turn left, I would use the command "Gee." To turn right, the command would be "Har." I would guide the mule with ropes attached to its harness and a "bit" in its mouth—this was the way to keep control of the mule. When I wanted it to stop, I would say "Wooh" or "Halt." To get it to go, I would say "Giddy up."

When plowing the field, there are different things to do to the earth to make sure the ground is in the right condition to take care of what is planted. Sometimes I used a certain plow to "turn over" the soil, meaning I was bringing the low earth to the top for planting. Sometimes I would use a certain plow to make rows. After the plants had sprouted and grown a little, I would use a certain plow to "lay by"—this means I would put a blanket of soft earth up close to the plants for warmth and protection.

Farm work is very, very hard work, but at harvest time, collecting what was sown always made me feel really good. Sometimes when I plowed the field I unearthed a bed of snakes. I had to quickly learn how to protect myself. The most effective way was to jump fast up on the mule's back and walk it away. Then I would get down, unhitch the plow, and turn the mule toward the snakes—and the mule would stomp the snakes to death. This happened to me three times when I was working the fields.

There are laws of the field; some of them are:

1. Never work a mule in the heat of the day.
2. Never work a mule without water close by so he can get water.
3. Never make the plow go so deep into the earth that the mule strains to pull the plow.
4. Never overload a wagon that the mule must pull.
5. Never walk a mule on asphalt or very hard earth without shoes on the mule. A mule has very, very tender hooves that damage easily.

A mule is a very smart and can be taught to do many things on his own without anyone guiding him, such as walking at a certain pace when harvesting tobacco. The tobacco croppers place green tobacco leaves in the sled, and after the sled is full, a mule can be taught to take it to the barn a mile away and return with an empty sled.

Hay is the food all mules eat. They also love corn on the cob and apples.

Hogs are a must-have for farmers. We had at least two hogs most of my life on the farm. All parts of the hog are used for meat. The side and thigh is where we get bacon. The ears are good eating; so are the feet. Southern people know how to cook the best pigs' feet. On New Year's Day, many Southerners will cook a hog's head with chitterlings, or "chitlins." These are the intestines of the hog. They stink very badly when cleaning or cooking them, but they are very tasty with hot corn bread.

Before the farmer slaughters the hog, he transfers the hog from its usual muddy, sloppy living pen to one built off the ground on a wooden platform; that's where he cleans up the hog. The hog is no longer fed dirty, sloppy food. Now he is fed fruits, berries, watermelon, and cantaloupe to help clean out the body. It takes about six weeks of this before slaughter day, which takes place somewhere between November and February.

When I was a child, all the boys were kept home from school on the day the slaughter was to take place so that they could help out with everything—it's a lot of hard work. First, the lady of the house would make a fire in the back of the house around two or more large pots of water. The men would sharpen knives and get rope ready. This may sound bad or cruel, but this is where meat comes from. The slaughter must be done right, or the meat is not good to eat.

When everything was in place, the men approached the hog pen. One would shoot the hog between the eyes or use a hammer to knock the hog out. Another man would stab the hog in the neck so as to bleed the hog thoroughly. Next, the process was to remove all the hair from the body using the boiling hot water in the pots. Next, the hog would be strung up with the ropes so the men could gut it—remove the inside parts of the hog. Every member knew his job, and everything worked out well. Everyone would share in the meat collection, and very little, if any, was wasted. The women would often grind some of the meat to eat for supper that very day.

Gathering eggs from the chickens was another story, because we did not get an egg every day. We boys would watch for the hen to go into the henhouse or chicken coop, and when she came out, we would race inside to see if there was an egg. Sometimes the hen would not lay her eggs in the coop because she wanted to sit on them in order to raise more chicks. So she would find a place in the nearby woods to lay her nest. Most times, we would find the eggs because we were hungry.

We were so very poor that a few times, we had no grease to cook the egg. On these occasions, we cooked with a small smear of Vaseline. This might sound unbelievable, but it's true—we did it. We used wild sap from certain trees as our chewing gum. We made toothpicks from certain tree branches. Dried corn was ground to make corn meal. We would make hoe cakes from plain corn meal and water. No butter was used, although sometimes Mother would make "crackling bread." This was done by mixing small bits of pig skin with the corn meal and water. If we bought the corn meal at the store, a bag would cost thirteen cents, and a bag of flour was eighteen cents.

Here's a list of other foods that we enjoyed, along with where we got the food.

Cucumbers	Our garden
Yams	Our garden
Squash	Our garden
Okra	Our garden
Pinto beans	General store
Butter beans	Our garden
Tomatoes	Our garden
Corn	Our garden
Collard greens	Our garden
Turnips	Our garden
Cabbage	Our garden
Neck bones	About seven to twelve cents per pound

at the general store

Rabbit   We would hunt

Squirrel   We would hunt

Raccoon   We would hunt

Pecans   Some days, this was our only meal

Peanuts   If we could find them

In late summer 1958 we moved out of Wagram for good. Things had started to change—we were living on farm land that was owned by hateful white owners. They wanted everyone who lived on the land to be active in the harvest work, even the boys who went to school. They wanted us boys to go out to the field as soon as we got home. Mommy did not like this "every day" order, so she made it known—and the land owners didn't like that. What got us evicted, though, was one Sunday afternoon when we boys, along with Inez (my sister Daisy's daughter), made a mistake—we pushed some big pipes into a ditch and then could not get them out again. When the workmen came to work that Monday, they saw foot tracks that led from our house directly to the ditch, and they reported what we had done to the land owner. He came to see my mother and ordered her to move immediately. To force us out quickly, the land owner had someone plow with a tractor as close to our house as he could. He cut up our garden and flower bed. The tractor even knocked over our clean clothes on the clothesline in the yard.

My brother Curtiss, who was in the twelfth grade at this time, had the position of school bus driver. He was responsible for picking up the students and taking them to school and then back home again. After school, he'd park the school bus at our house. After we were evicted, however, he had nowhere to park to the bus. He had to give up that job, and the school gave the bus route to another student.

Two days later, we moved to Aberdeen, North Carolina, with my sister Daisy and her husband, Bob Byrd—a very, very good brother-in-law. That August I started school at Berkley High School in Aberdeen; although it was called a "high school," it held both upper and lower grades. I was in about the fifth or sixth grade when the astronaut John Glenn went into space and circled the earth for a few hours.

Aberdeen was nice, but we lived on Pink Hill Farm, which was a long way from school. No bus came that far. So my little brother, Johnnie, and

I would have to get up early to be ready to leave with Mr. Bob, as he was called, when he left for work. He passed Berkley High School on his way and would drop us at the school every day at 6:30 a.m. We would wait in the halls until school started.

On the trip home, we could catch the school bus that would go as close to our house as possible, and then we would walk the long country road to get home. The only problem was that we had to pass two houses on that road where the residents would call us nigger every day—they would wait by the road for us. Sometimes we would dodge them by going through the woods, but in the woods there were all types of snakes (rattlesnakes, black snakes) and even wolves. We never carried any protection. Along the first part of our walk, after getting off the bus, there was a white family who was very nice and never called us names. In fact, if the man was home, he would walk with us past the ones who gave us trouble. When he was with us, they never said anything. They would see him with us and go back to their houses.

Mr. Bob and Daisy's house was too small for all of us, so we moved into an old gas station–like place on Highway 1 in Aberdeen. Mommy looked for a real house, which she found a few months later, not too far away. It was on a long, desolate highway—the closest house about a mile and a half away. We had no phone, TV, radio, or electricity, but we made it. I did not get much schooling at this time. My mother had a male friend named Sam, who was one of Mr. Bob's friends.

Sam was nice. He would talk to us and tell us about his life as a "slave." He actually worked for a sharecropper and could come and go at will, but he worked all his life and was never paid one dollar. He had a room to live in and could cook and eat all he wanted, but he said he never saw any money for his work. I remember his saying that he was not mad about that, because he knew that the ones who had enslaved him would one day get what they deserved.

Sam died soon after we met. I sure missed his coming by because at this time, my brothers Lester, Curtiss, Willie, and Robert L. were in New York City. I was the big man at home with Mommy and little brother, Johnnie. I needed a male figure to show me things, and we didn't know my dad's whereabouts at this time.

For me, 1960 was very much like the years 1958 and 1959—I was growing into manhood with not much to do. I had no one to grow up with, other than my brother Johnnie. Going fishing was very big part of my life. Some days I would get work, driving a farm tractor in the field for two dollars for the day. I had nothing, so this was good money. At least I could buy myself a soda and honey bun, which I loved.

This was the time when I started writing poems and short stories to keep busy. Unfortunately, I lost these writings over time and no longer have them to share. I've heard that once you lose or misplace your writing, you cannot recoup any of it in your memory. I cannot recall the poems and stories now because so many years have passed, but I wrote quite a few.

The year 1961 was a trying one in my young manhood. I would turn sixteen years old in April. All my older brothers had left home for a new life in New York City, so now it was just Mommy, my youngest brother, Johnnie, and me. We now lived in Laurinburg, North Carolina. Johnnie would turn twelve in March. Our mother did the very best she could for us. We still had to use an outhouse because we had no indoor plumbing. All the houses in our section were the same style row house. Our address was 312 Bridge Street. This was our first house with an address. All the other houses where we lived had general delivery post office boxes. We had to walk at least a mile or more to pick up our mail.

Johnnie and I attended Lincoln High School in Laurinburg. We walked one mile to school each day, carrying our books.

The hallways at school during change of class or at lunchtime were deathly quiet. There was no running in the hallways and no gum chewing in school at all. Students could be sent home for little things, such as whistling inside the school. But there were always fights among the boy students, usually over a girl or name-calling.

Anyone who wanted to get a girlfriend had to dress sharp, have a tall crew cut–style haircut, and always be ready to carry the girl's books. She might say yes; she might say no. If she said no, then the boy knew to leave her alone—in those days, daddies would come after anyone who was bothering their daughters.

The dress code was far different back then than it is today. The school system in the South, even though it was segregated, held a high standard on dress and grooming. Male teachers wore ties and starched shirts; female teachers wore mostly flower or plaid dresses. Female teachers were not allowed to wear pants.

I had very little to wear to school. I missed many, many days because of being too ashamed to go to school with holes in my shoes or wearing the same shirt or pants week after week. So I would wash the one pair of pants and shirt I had and use them for two to three days, and then I'd just stay home the next two days. I lost out on so much. But somehow, I was still liked by my teacher. I was mostly a C student, with a few Bs here and there. I was not up to par with my homework because of the time I missed from school. When I was home, I mostly sat around doing nothing—we had no TV or radio. Sometimes my friend James Rush would play hooky and come by my house, and we would shoot marbles or pitch horseshoes. These were two commonly played games by young men at that time. We would never go in town, because we knew the truant officers would be there to pick up kids playing hooky.

I'd wanted to be part of the football team at Lincoln but could not because of my attendance record. One afternoon, however, a player did not show up for practice, and I asked if I could fill in for him—and I was given the okay. That was the last time I played, and I never asked again. I was talked into running a play that I knew nothing about and was hit from two sides at the same time—I was almost knocked out. After that, I was dizzy for days. I gave up the idea of playing football, but I still love the game today.

Things changed for me in February 1961—changed my life forever. My mother was receiving thirty-two dollars a month from the welfare department to help her pay expenses. The rent on the house where we lived was twelve dollars a month. The welfare department told her they would cut off her welfare payments unless she allowed them to send me to a boys school. They thought this would keep me out of trouble because I was not attending school regularly.

They wanted to meet with Mommy and me at the welfare office on a Friday. First, I said I wouldn't go because I knew I had done nothing wrong. My only crime was that I could not afford clothes for school. But the love for my mother made me want to obey. At the meeting in an old courthouse, Mommy and I sat down with two white women, and they told her that they were sending me to Morrison Training School for Boys in Hoffman, North Carolina, twenty-five miles from home.

I wanted to know why they were taking me away from my mother, but they only said I had no choice in the matter. So I said, "Okay, I'll just run away before you can send me." After I said that, one of the women went into another room and came back with a policeman. The policeman told my mother that the judge said he could lock me up in jail until I could be sent to the training school.

I wanted to fight, but I looked at Mommy and saw how upset and worried she looked, and I just gave in. I gave in because I didn't want to worry Mommy, and I allowed them to enslave me in a jail cell, although I had committed no crime.

At this time in my life, all my aunts and uncles were alive. My aunt Elnora lived nearby, and she would also come to the fence of the jail and call to me to say hello and to see how I was being treated. One day in April 1961 when she came by, she said that she was not feeling well and was going to the hospital. About a week later, Mommy told me that Aunt Elnora had died. This hurt me very much. Aunt Elnora—we called her Aunt Nora—was Mommy's backbone. She helped all of us. The last words she spoke to me on her last visit to the jail were: "Sonny, you stay out of trouble now. Bye-bye."

It was a big funeral. I was given time out to attend, without bond or escort. I could have run away but my mother would have been blamed, and I could not do it to her. While I was out, a funny thing happened. My cousin Jerry Blue (Aunt Eva's son, who was my age) had come down from New York to attend the funeral. He went uptown, and the police accused him of shoplifting some Royal Crown hair grease from a store. He ended up in the same jail cell that I had just left. I would have company when I went back! It made me happy that I would be able to talk with someone who was familiar to me.

After the funeral, when everyone had left, I talked to Mommy and told her not to worry, that I would take care of myself. I kissed her and walked across the street to the jail so they could lock me back up. As I entered my cell, I said, "Hi, Jerry. I'm home."

Early May 1961, I was taken to Morrison Training School for Boys in Hoffman, North Carolina, which was not far from the house of my father, Willie McLean. Everyone who knew my mother and father would say that I looked just like him, but I had my mother's kind, giving ways.

My mother rode in the car with the white woman to take me to Morrison. Again, I could have gotten away, but my mother was my life, and I could not hurt her in any way. Morrison was like a retreat—four or five brick buildings where boys of different ages stayed. There was a school building (like all other schools, red brick), a gym, and a football field. I was housed in a building for boys who were fifteen and sixteen years old. We had a house mother and house father—a married couple. They stayed with us around the clock. The father was the only one who would enter our sleeping section. The mother was the one who made sure our clothes were sent out to be washed. She also made our food, talked to us, and made sure we did not fight (but there were plenty of fights). When a rule was broken, we could expect corporal punishment. The house father used a thick board-like paddle to our behinds. For example, if we were caught smoking, we were told to bend over and would get three to five hard whacks on our butts—and they hurt. Peeing in bed called for five whacks, and then we were sent to what was called the "skunk ward" for two nights, with only a blanket across bed springs. I spent a few nights there until I said to myself, *Enough is enough.* I helped myself stop wetting the bed by not drinking fluids or eating watermelon after a certain time. At last, I got off skunk ward.

At Morrison, every student would go to regular school from 8:00 a.m. until noon or from 1:00 p.m. until 5:00 p.m. All in-between hours were spent working in the field. We made about fifteen cents an hour. We could keep eight cents, but the rest was put aside for us to use when we went home or were released. There were so many bright minds going to waste at this school—kids who had so much talent, so much to give. There were singers, boxers, poem writers, music players, dancers—you name it. But there was no one to guide them. There also were the crime-movers who knew, at that young age, how the cheat, steal, con, rob, and even kill. I had to learn how to avoid these types of boys, as I didn't want to be involved in the things they were doing; I didn't want problems.

Thankfully, in September 1961 I was moved from Morrison to a school for boys and girls, O'Berry Training School, in Goldsboro, North Carolina. I now was more than eighty miles from home. O'Berry was mostly for boys and girls who would not attend school regularly, had problems at home, or had a handicap and the parents could not take care of them.

Some of the kids were very sick mentally but nonviolent. They needed around-the-clock care and attention. For instance, when some of them needed to use the bathroom, someone in charge would need to be right there to flush the waste right away, because the kids' minds would tell them it was okay to reach in the toilet and grab their bowel movement. Guys like me—those who were able to function without help or guidance—were asked to help out with those who needed special help. We were known as toilet policemen.

But my favorite job was to assist young guys who could not write or read. I would write letters to their loved ones for them, always saying only what they told me to say. When they received a letter, I would take them to a quiet spot and read it to them. I never would repeat to anyone else what was written in the letter.

For recreation we would go swimming or play marbles or horseshoes. We had basketball games on Saturday, Wednesday, and Friday nights. Our school would play other schools. Anyone who had a girlfriend at the school could sit with her on the benches. After the game, the girls went out one side of the gym, and the boys went out the other side. At the school we had what were called canteen hours every other Saturday. For three hours, boys and girls could dance to rock-and-roll music and eat candy and popcorn. No slow dancing, holding hands, or outside secret talks was allowed.

I had a girlfriend while I was at O'Berry. She was light skinned with nice, long, curly hair. All the so-called popular guys would not be around her because she was cross-eyed. She had lost her mother very young, did not know her dad, and had no brothers or sisters. At the time I met her, she was about fourteen or fifteen. She told me that the school forced the girls to drink a solution at breakfast to ensure none of the girls became pregnant. She asked me to remember, if I ever left the school, to come back for her when she turned eighteen years old. I don't remember how I responded, but I left O'Berry in August 1962, and I never heard from her again.

Also at the school was the Vaughan family—Wallace, William, Joseph (Jo-Baby), and Nancy. Wallace and I were the same age. Jo-Baby was the youngest. Their mother and father were drunkards, and the kids had been placed at the school by the welfare department.

Jo-Baby was a problem with everyone, always picking fights. William was cool. Wallace never bothered anyone. Jo-Baby started problems with me. I went to both his brothers and asked them to stop him, or we would put on the gloves. Both brothers said to me, "If you whip his butt, we are not jumping in, because we told him to leave fights alone." But Jo-Baby kept it up. On Saturdays, anyone who had a beef with someone could voice it to the person in charge of the dorm. In turn, he would talk to that person, and then there would be one of two choices for the person: get the paddle seven times, or put on the boxing gloves and step in the ring with the one who had named him as causing trouble.

I reported Jo-Baby, and he should have asked for the paddle, but being cocky and self-assured, he chose to put on the gloves and fight me. A big mistake! We had three rounds, two minutes each. After the second round, Jo-Baby said, "I quit." He had one closed eye, a bloody nose, and a bloody lip. He never bothered me again.

One day, out of the blue, William Vaughan, Jo Baby, and I, along with two other brothers, decided to run away. It was a Saturday in October 1961. We had no plan, no food, no money, no clothes—and no sense. We five fools ran off into the woods. I was wearing sandals, a dashiki shirt, and thin khaki pants. We didn't stop to think that it would get cold at night—we just ran off. I thought we could make it to Laurinburg. We were some seventy to eighty miles away—five nappy-headed boys with no direction at all. We walked, then we ran through the woods. We would not go on the highway, because we knew someone from the school would be looking for us. As night fell, it started to get colder and colder, but nobody wanted to give up and go back.

We spotted an empty barn in a field, and I said, "Let's go in for the night." We were hungry and had nothing to eat. We had a box of matches, so we made a fire. And we tried to make popcorn from some old corn that was left behind in the barn, but it didn't work. So all night we starved, couldn't sleep, and almost froze to death.

The next day, Sunday, we start walking again, this time on the road—we had only gone about three miles from the school. Now we came into a town called Mount Olive. We saw a country store and tried to steal some candy through an open window, but the owner caught us. We ran, but he and some other people chased us and caught two of the boys—but not me, because I was in the lead, running down the railroad tracks. When I saw that two of the boys had been caught, I returned and let them take me, too. We were taken to the police station and some teachers from the school came to get us and return us to the school, where we all were put on punishment.

Our new house was between the courthouse and the town. It was near an A&P supermarket, and when I would get hungry, I would go to the rear of the store, where they put out fruit and dented cans that could not be sold, and I would bring them home. I'd wash the fruit and cut out the spoiled parts and enjoy a fruit dinner. But I had competition—it was first come, first served on most days. When there were no throw-outs from the A&P, I would go inside and wait for a chance to steal some cold cuts, cookies, or canned meats. But after I did so, I would not feel good about it. I guess I knew it was wrong to steal, and I stopped as fast as I started.

I started making rabbit boxes and would set two boxes a day, looking to trap a rabbit to eat. My mother knew how to cook a rabbit and make it taste just like chicken. She would make thick brown gravy and serve rice and field peas with it. But one day, I had a rabbit trapped in my rabbit box and when I opened the trap door to remove it, he was looking up at me with big, wide eyes and flapping his ears. I took that to mean he was asking to be set free. I remember dropping the box and the door broke off. Away he hopped, and I never set another trap or ate rabbit after that encounter.

I turned my attention to fishing for a meal. Leaving my house very early in the morning, I would go to the nearby creek and by eight or nine o'clock, I would have enough fish for breakfast, lunch, and dinner. I felt good eating what I worked hard to catch, instead of something I'd stolen.

As much as we depended on our chickens for eggs and a chicken dinner on the farm, there were other creatures that wanted our chickens for a meal of their own. We always had to protect our investment, day and night. By day, we always were on the lookout for the chicken hawk that would make daily rounds to snatch a chicken from the yard and make a clean getaway. We lost a few chickens this way. The hawk was very fast when he came in to snatch the chickens. Most times, we only saw feathers flying around, and we'd look up in the sky and see him flying off with our chicken. The best way to protect the chicken yard, whenever we noticed our chickens acting strange, was to get our gun and fire a few shots in the air, even if we did not see a hawk. We knew he was somewhere close because he was the only thing that could make all the chickens in the yard upset at the same time. Somehow, they knew when the hawk was on the prowl.

At night, there were two creatures that worried us the most. The fox was sly—yes, he would watch the chicken house for days before he made his move. He knew somehow that the family was less active in the early hours—from 3:00 a.m. until dawn. He would check for the weak spots in the henhouse, but he was smart enough to make sure he had an escape route if he was detected. He would try to make two ways in so that he would have a way out. He would dig a little each night under the house until he had a tunnel large enough to fit his body. Also, he would test the makeup of the chicken house for the weak boards. Remember the saying, sly as a fox. When he was ready, he moved very quickly and low to the ground. As you might know, all fowl—chickens, ducks, geese—sleep with their heads and necks tucked under their wings. So unless they are touched, most times they will stay that way until morning. The fox seemed to know this. He would try to make his move to get his chicken and then get out before he woke the rooster. The rooster was king of the yard. Even the fox didn't want any part of Mr. Red Rooster.

The rooster has spurs on the side of each leg that can rip a man's leg wide open, and he will fight man or animal to protect his harem of chickens. We would tie a noisemaker on a string to the rooster's leg so we would know when he was near; then we could come and go without being attacked.

All roosters crow at the break of dawn. Without fail, they would always be up and ready, most times on a fence post but sometimes atop the barn or house. The chickens, though, were usually quiet at night, so when we would hear the chickens make noise in the coop, we knew there was a fox or other night animal around that was trying to get our chickens. That's why every house would keep a dog loose in the yard at night and one tied near the chicken coop.

Another problem at night was the opossum. This creature is an egg-eater as well as a chicken-eater. He could get into the chicken coop much easier than the fox, and if we caught him inside, he would play dead. But if we caught him off guard—such as if we were hunting in the woods at night—he would give us a silly grin. And if we got too close to him, he would leap on us to bite us—he was protecting his nest.

Next, there were weasels and black snakes, both of which love chicken eggs. Once I caught a black snake with an egg halfway into its mouth. I just toyed with it before I killed it, because I knew it was harmless at that point and could do nothing to me.

We also had to build a strong pen for our hogs and make sure to water and feed them often. If we didn't, they would find a way to get out. Most of the time we could find them and get them back, but not always. We might lose them to a wild beast in the woods, or someone else would find them, and our loss would be their gain.

These animals were the poor man's investment. We needed to keep something to trade off; for example, we might trade ten chickens for a baby pig, or some eggs for sugar. But if we did not work hard to protect our belongings, then there would be nothing for us to trade. Farm life was hard, but it taught us how to have the best time of our life if we worked hard enough.

I had learned to dance and was an expert with all the dances. Girls told me that I was a good dancer, but girls who danced with me once would hesitate the next time—they said I danced too fast and they couldn't keep up. I mastered all the dances that were popular at that time—the Slop, the Twist, the Pony, the Slide, the Alligator, the Scoot, the Swing, the Watusi, and the Slow Drag. Many more dances were popular, and we all learned them because that's all teenagers had to do when they socialized. Sure, we had football, basketball, softball, and riding bikes, but we wanted to be in a mixed gender crowd sometimes.

I also loved to read and write, and I would read any book I could get my hands on, except books about witchcraft or evil stuff. I stayed away from such reading. My choice was usually history or nature books. Writing was fun for me. I could do poems and songs. In fact, today I still have three songs that I penned about that time. People who read some of my writings said I had great potential, but I didn't want to be popular or rich for fear it would change my outlook on life. I feel many people spend a lifetime living the life they are not. It's best for your soul to be free of agents or handlers who tell you how to go about your life.

All schools in North Carolina in the 1950s and 1960s were segregated, which included having a segregated faculty. It was either a colored school or a white school. All books used by everyone, however, had photos in them that were of white kids or adults. Photos of black people were not allowed. When white educators would visit a colored school, all students were briefed on how to greet or speak to them. We were told to say, "Yes, ma'am" or "Yes, sir."

For dinner in school—it was not called lunch back then—all students would sing a grace song together before eating. One song was as follows:

> God is great and God is good,
> And we thank him for our food.
> Bow our heads, must all be fed.
> Give us, Lord, our daily bread.
> Give us, Lord, our daily bread.
> Amen.

Food at school was not free. Lunch/dinner was ten cents a day, plus three cents a day for a small container of milk or juice. The teacher would collect the money for the week each Monday. The students who could not afford to buy lunch/dinner at school—and there were many—could bring a sandwich and buy milk for three cents and join others in a special room. My brother Lester and I spent many, many days in such a room because Mommy just did not have the money for us to buy a meal. When she did have something, we would allow our baby brother, Johnnie, to buy the lunch/dinner, and we would go without. But we knew Mommy would have something on the stove when we arrived home from school. Most days she would only have cooked dried peas and corn bread, with a glass of sugar water. We were always happy to get even that. Some days when I got home from school, I would need to go in the garden and cut some okra, wash it, fry it, and make a corn-bread cake before I could eat.

During dinner/lunch in school, there were strict rules. Every student who bought lunch/dinner got the same meal. If they did not like it, they would just go hungry. The teachers controlled the order in the room. No student—girl or boy—could sit at a table with a hat on. We could use only one hand to eat with. There was no yelling, no whistling, no elbows on the table allowed. Each class would enter and leave together—this rule was for grades as high as eighth and ninth.

Beginning about the third grade, before class started each morning two things would take place: the first thing was that the teacher would select one boy student and one girl student to go around the room and check students' personal hygiene. Did the student have clean ears or dirty ears? Clean hands or dirty hands? Hair combed or not combed? Did he or she smell dirty or smell clean? Was he or she wearing clean clothes or dirty clothes?

Each student's name was on a chart by the teacher's desk for all to see. The purpose was to embarrass a student who was dirty so that he or she would clean up before coming to class.

The second thing was devotion time. Each student was asked to say a Bible verse, usually from the Ten Commandments in the Bible. Most of the time, the same verse was repeated time after time. Some students were very shy and spoke in a low tone, and the teacher would sometimes yell at them to get it out of them.

During the cold months, about fifteen minutes before class was over for the day, the teacher would select one boy and one girl to pass out all coats from the closet. As this was being done, the room would be totally quiet—not a sound. Corporal punishment was widespread in all schools in the southern states. Every teacher was given the right to exercise what he or she thought was just. From misspelled words to talking in class, from cheating on tests to not having a pencil or notepaper, a student could get a certain number of whacks with a hard ruler on the palm of each hand, directly in front of the class. However, any student caught laughing at the one being punished would also be brought up front.

I remember once in my sixth-grade class, my teacher, Mrs. Heading, got me good, and there was nothing I could do about it. She was teaching the class, and for some reason, I remembered a quiz from a book or magazine that told which state in the United States produced the majority of cotton—it was Texas.

So out of the blue, in the middle of the class, I raised my hand. Mrs. Heading, thinking I was about to comment on the lesson she was teaching, called on me.

But I made a big mistake, and I paid for it later. I said, "Mrs. Heading, since you are so smart, I bet you know where the most cotton is grown." She looked straight at me, and I knew I was in trouble. When the time came to be dismissed for dinner, she told another student to escort the class to the lunch hall to eat. She stood in the doorway as all the students filed out, and just as my turn came, she grabbed me and told me to wait right there. As the class left the hallway and was a distance away where they could not hear, she gave me a back-handed slap so hard, I thought my head had exploded. I saw stars of all colors. I was hurting, my mouth was bleeding, and my face felt like it was on fire.

She said, "You'd better never embarrass me again like that. Now, you walk in the hall, with no tears but with a smile. If you say anything, I will do it again when school is over today."

When I opened the door to the lunch hall, all eyes were on me. Everyone knew I was hurting; they could see my face. I had to sit and eat like this; I was hurt. Mrs. Heading looked right at me all the time.

I could not go to school for few days after being hit like that. I must admit, while I was home, spitting blood, I would look in the corner at my mother's .22 caliber rifle, and bad thoughts were in my mind. I never told Mommy what had happened. I loved her too much to worry her. I didn't even dare tell my brother Lester; he always had a bad temper. I never hated Mrs. Heading for what she did to me, but I never forgot. I left Shaw High School soon after and never saw her again.

Two articles of clothing that students tried to avoid wearing to school in those days were overall pants and brogaine boots. Today in 2011, these same items are worn by many and cost lots of money. Back in the 1950s, anyone who wore them would be laughed at. The most the boots cost would be a dollar-fifty to three dollars. The overalls cost about five dollars.

While I was at O'Berry Training School, I was asked to stay as a staff member after I turned twenty-one. I had no intention of doing that at all. So 1962 started out well for me, although I didn't know I would be a New Yorker by the end of the year. At this time my mother had moved back to Aberdeen, North Carolina, to be near my sister, Daisy. I was given two weeks' leave from the school to spend time with Mommy. It just so happened that one week after coming home, my brother Lester came to visit. He had his girlfriend, Doris, and her sister, Faye, with him. He was only twenty years old, but he had driven his 1959 Chevy Impala all the way to North Carolina by himself. One morning, he said to me, "Claudie, you want to come to New York. I don't want my brother to go back to that school." I remember he also said I must ask Mommy first.

So I asked her. First, she said no, and I was okay with that. I was not going to disobey. But later that day, she called me to her and said, "Son, if you go up the road"—to New York—"you take care of yourself, and stay out of trouble." Then she looked me straight in the eyes and said, "If you ever get a girl in bearing way, you stick with her, marry her, and take care of both. I am holding you to that." Then she kissed me on the cheek and said, "You can go, son. I love you. Be sure to take care of Lester also."

~ENTERING MANHOOD~

I arrived in New York City on August 15, 1962. I was shocked to find out that Lester had no room for me. He and Doris had a one-bedroom apartment at 810 St. John's Place. So I took myself to my brother Curtiss's house. He did not know I was coming. He had a wife, Betty, and young son, Tony, to feed and take care of. My sister-in-law Betty truly welcomed me warmly into her home.

Lester was working as a security guard at Brooklyn Hospital. He got me my first job. I was underage to work full time, so they gave me a job in the kitchen from 4:00 p.m. to 8:00 p.m. It was nice, clean, and I had very nice coworkers. Lester would pick me up at Curtiss and Betty's house at 646 Herkimer Street. (Now, a boys and girls high school is on that site.) Even on nights when Lester had a date (and he had many), he would never be late to pick me up from work, and he always made sure I got home. One afternoon, however, I got busted for eating on the job. Our supervisor had made it very clear that we could eat all we wanted, free of charge, after all the patients' floors were served but not until then. I was not hungry when I did it, so I don't know why I broke this rule.

My job that day was to release a hot ball-like object into a tin pan, and the plate of food would be placed on top, and then a cover would be placed over the food to help keep the food hot until it reached the patient's room. Also that day, I was serving desserts. When I saw the supervisor go out one door, I took a chance and bit into a piece of cherry pie. Before I could swallow it, the supervisor walked in from another door, right in front of where I stood.

I was sent to the office and told I would not be fired but would be demoted to mopping the floor. Embarrassed, I did not want to do that, because girls would see me and laugh at me. I made a bad choice—I said, "I prefer to quit." The supervisor said, "Go home and think about it, and see how you feel tomorrow."

The next day my mind was the same—I could not face my coworkers when mopping the floors. My supervisor begged me to reconsider. I wouldn't, but I have regretted not doing so ever since. They gave me my $69.14 payout, and with that, my job at Brooklyn Hospital was history.

After Brooklyn Hospital, I found other jobs, mostly factory work. It was often six weeks here before layoff; two weeks there before layoff. I was paid eight cents an hour, which amounted to thirty-two dollars for a forty-hour week. I had to pay eight dollars to rent a room, where there was no cooking allowed. I believe I made about $360 for all of 1962. I returned home to visit Mommy between jobs. Also, the school had been hounding Mommy to tell them where I was and for her to convince me to return to school. Mommy explained that I had not committed a crime; I had just dropped out of school. Also, my brother Curtiss sent a letter to the school authorities, saying that I was in his custody and was no longer required by law to attend school. After that, they left me alone. I revisited the school two years later to say hello and let the teachers know how I was doing. They all gave me a thumbs-up and said they expected me to do well.

Two months after beginning a new life in Brooklyn, New York, I returned to Aberdeen, North Carolina, in October 1962 to visit Mommy, my baby brother, Johnnie, and other members of my family. Suddenly, I was somewhat of a celebrity. I tried to talk like a New Yorker. Everywhere I would go, I told people that I lived in New York—this was a big thing. A boy from New York with a car got attention from the girls. But even without a car, if a girl found out a boy was from New York, he had it made.

During this visit I wanted to go fishing, and as I had done for years, I went fishing in a muddy creek, along with about ten other guys and my brother Johnnie. We were having fun and laughing, and I told them about the bright lights and big city of New York. Suddenly, one of the guys said, "Look, the game warden is here." I had no concern with this because we were fishing in a creek, not in a standing pond—in a creek, a fishing license was not needed. The game warden greeted us and asked, "How's the fishing going?" I am not sure that anyone responded to his question, because he walked closer to me and repeated the question.

I said, "Nothing yet."

He said, "Why don't you check your pole. You might have a fish on the hook."

This was my mistake; I bent down to pick up my pole to check it, and right away the game warden said, "Boy, can I see your fishing license? You need a license to fish in the waters of Aberdeen."

I was stunned and shocked. I couldn't believe it—after all, I used to fish in this spot morning and night, day after day, without any problems at all—and I'd only been away in New York for two months. Why had he asked no one but me?

Later, I found out that none of my friends had picked up a fishing pole, so the game warden could not ask for a license from any of them because he could not prove that they were fishing. I also realized that I got his attention because of the way I was dressed—a white shirt, shiny black pants, and shoes that were spit-shined. I wore a gold-plated watch and ring, shades, and had cigarettes in my shirt pocket and a rich-looking straw hat on my head. No one dressed like that in Aberdeen, a slow town with a population of five hundred. I stood out, dressed like that while fishing in a muddy creek. The warden said to me, "Boy, I got to take you in for fishing without a license. You will be fined." I protested, telling him that my mother worked for his mother, scrubbing her floors. I also insisted I had broken no law; I had fished in this same spot for years.

Still, I went with him to his boss's office in town. My brother went to get our mother. All the other guys followed behind us, going to the office to watch over me. I was given a fine of $23.50—it was the only money I had for bus fare to return to New York. Now I was broke and had no choice but to sell my watch and ring. I got a total of twenty-five dollars for them and was able to buy a ticket to New York City.

Later, I learned that I should never have been fined. The fishing license law applied to everyone twenty-one years old or older; I was a mere seventeen years old. I still have the fine in my records of things of the past. However, that was the way things were done in the South—at that time, injustice was everywhere. Black people could not sit at a soda fountain and sip a soda because, first of all, they usually would not be sold one because they were black. And if they were able to buy a soda, they were not permitted to drink it inside; they had to go out back to drink it.

It was the same thing with ice cream cones. Whites could buy ice cream inside the shop, but blacks could only order from a side window or back door. We knew it was wrong, but for the most part, we lived with it. We couldn't complain about it to anyone—the sheriff was the judge, the prosecutor, the hangman, the city lawyer, and the councilman; he had the final say. This was life in the South at that time. It was the accepted way; we knew not to question it.

The year 1963 rocked in hard and fast, and the city of New York was about to change. The Beach Boys, Sam Cooke, and many more singers were about to be upended by a group out of Liverpool, England, called the Beatles.

I was babysitting Tony while Betty and Curtiss worked. However, I worked a few more factory jobs early in 1963 and rented the hall room from Curtiss and Betty. I felt a need to move up a notch on my own. On Memorial Day 1963, I left Curtiss and Betty's house for good. They both had been very kind to me during my entire stay. Betty cooked for me, and when she did the wash, she always did my clothes as well. When she cleaned, she cleaned my room also.

I moved in with Lester and Doris, who now were living at 330 Tompkins Avenue in a large apartment. Here, I had my own entrance to the apartment so I could get to my room without having to walk through the apartment. I was more on my own, as I had to make my own meals or eat out in restaurants. By this time Lester had changed hospital jobs; he now worked at a new hospital, Maimonides, at Forty-Eighth Street and Tenth Avenue in Brooklyn. He was able to get jobs for me, my fiancée, Mary, and his fiancée, Rachael. I worked as a porter, Mary worked as a central supply clerk, and Rachael worked in the laundry.

On November 22, 1963, I was at work, waxing a floor, when I heard on a radio in one of the rooms that the president had been shot. I went to the nurses' station and told them what I had just heard. At first, no one believed me, but the radio kept repeating the news. Soon, everyone knew what had happened, and the whole floor went crazy.

The South in the 1950s and '60s was a time of segregation, and everyone knew their place. Blacks knew the things they could or could not do. They always said "Yes, sir" or "No, sir" to a white man, but the white man never reciprocated with equal respect. Blacks had to enter a store at the rear, through the colored door. If a black man was walking down the street in town and a white woman was walking in his direction, he would have to cross to the other side or step in the gutter until she passed. And he would never speak to her; speaking to a white woman could get a colored man lynched very quickly. Victims were often tortured and mutilated before being killed. Sometimes they were burned alive to give onlookers something to cheer about. These were called public hangings. The same people who agreed to uphold the law actually broke the law themselves. Men, women, and children were lynched for no other reason than being colored.

A group called the Ku Klux Klan, also known as the "night riders," was feared. The group was made up of people who were so-called respected citizens by day but who incited terror by night. Colored people in my neighborhood were insulted daily, but with the fear of violence and death always near, many just turned the other cheek to survive.

The Jim Crow laws in the South at that time mandated segregation. Coloreds could legally be treated in any way without the perpetrators being punished by the courts. This was the reason for the Great Migration— African Americans leaving the South to escape racism. Race riots erupted all across the country.

I never was beaten up by whites; I was only called names. I picked cotton and worked the farm for a white man, mostly trouble-free. My family was helped in many, many ways by whites, while racism was going on around us. I believe one reason for this was because we tried to avoid trouble. We lived deep in the country at this time, with no car, no telephone—just a mother with very young boys in the house. In many black families in the South, after the older boys left home for the large cities, very few returned to stay. They would visit on holidays or if there was a death in the family, but most of them would say, "I am never going back South to live." However, in the late 1970s, many did return South to build homes of their own. Even I considered that idea at one time. But city life had transformed me. I was now used to a fast-paced way of life, and returning to a slower lifestyle didn't appeal to me. I don't think I would have been able to return to farm life, not in the way I'd been used to. Everything had taken on such modern ways that I would have been lost. However, when I did return home for visits, I always found joy in looking over the fields where I once toiled in the cotton from sunup till sundown. I enjoyed hearing the birds sing the lovely songs—and the mockingbird has quite a few songs that are just mind-boggling.

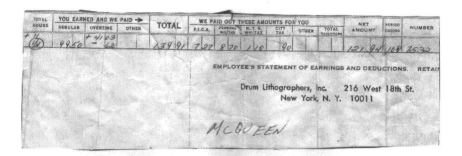

TOTAL HOURS	YOU EARNED AND WE PAID →			TOTAL	WE PAID OUT THESE AMOUNTS FOR YOU						NET AMOUNT	PERIOD ENDING	NUMBER
	REGULAR	OVERTIME	OTHER		F.I.C.A.	FEDERAL WH/TAX	N.Y.S. WH/TAX	CITY TAX	OTHER	TOTAL DEDUCTIONS			
40	4950	4103 62		139 91	7 07	8 70	1 00	90			121 94	1-18 8532

EMPLOYEE'S STATEMENT OF EARNINGS AND DEDUCTIONS. RETAI

Drum Lithographers, Inc.   216 West 18th St.
New York, N. Y.   10011

MCQUEEN

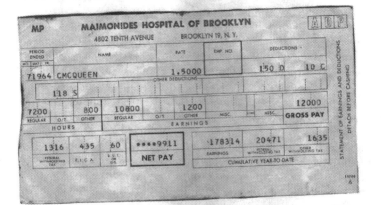

MP   MAIMONIDES HOSPITAL OF BROOKLYN   A D P

4802 TENTH AVENUE   BROOKLYN 19, N. Y.

PERIOD ENDED MO DAY YR	NAME	RATE	EMP. NO.	DEDUCTIONS
71964	CMCQUEEN	1.5000	150 D	10 C

OTHER DEDUCTIONS
118 S

REGULAR	O/T OTHER	REGULAR	O/T OTHER	MISC	MISC	GROSS PAY
HOURS		EARNINGS				
7200	800	10800	1200			12000

FEDERAL WITHHOLDING TAX	F.I.C.A.	S.U.T. OR DIS.	NET PAY	EARNINGS	FEDERAL TAX	OTHER WITHHOLDING TAX
1316	435	80	****9911	178314	20471	1635

CUMULATIVE YEAR-TO-DATE

STATEMENT OF EARNINGS AND DEDUCTIONS   DETACH BEFORE CASHING

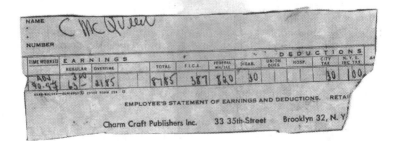

NAME C McQueen

NUMBER

TIME WORKED	EARNINGS			DEDUCTIONS							
	REGULAR	OVERTIME	TOTAL	F.I.C.A.	FEDERAL WH/TAX	DISAB.	UNION DUES	HOSP.	CITY TAX	N.Y.S. INC TAX	
40 40·97	3 30 63 50	2185	8785	387	820	30			30	100	

EMPLOYEE'S STATEMENT OF EARNINGS AND DEDUCTIONS. RETAI

Charm Craft Publishers Inc.   33 35th Street   Brooklyn 32, N. Y.

I was working at Maimonides Hospital as a porter in the housekeeping department, from 7:00 a.m. until 3:00 p.m. In order to be at work on time, I had to be up by 5:00 a.m., leave home by 5:30, and walk about thirteen blocks to get the A-train at the Kingston and Troop Avenue station on Fulton Street. I would ride to Hoyt Street station, change to the RR train at the Thirty-Sixth Street station, change to the T-train at the Fort Hamilton Avenue station, and walk seven blocks to the hospital. I always arrived between 6:35 and 6:45 a.m. every day; I was never late.

In February 1964, a large snowstorm shut down the city. Bus and train service was at a standstill. Large banks of snow were everywhere. My entire department at the hospital was kept on overtime, twenty-four hours at a time, because we were responsible for snow removal. But this was good because for each twenty-four-hour shift I worked, I earned a full week's pay.

The hospital work was nice, clean work. The department I was assigned to was mixed races, as well as young and older people. I was always invited to house parties on the weekend, although I was very reluctant to accept an invitation. This was mostly because at that time, gangs worked different neighborhoods. They would ask any young man why he was in their neighborhood and say, "Are you here to pick up our girls?" They might then attack the boy, depending how he was dressed, how he walked, and how he answered their questions.

I was stopped twice by a gang called the Chaplins. Their color was beige—beige khaki pants and beige floppy hat. Their shirts always were out at the waist. They wore sunglasses year-round. Their turf was between Greene Avenue and Fulton Street and between Tompkins and Lewis

Avenue. They used brass knuckles, short chains, pipes, and zip guns. Zip guns were made using a short pipe, rubber band, nail, and a piece of wood. All of this would be taped to the pipe to hold it together. These things were very deadly.

The Beatles were very hot at this time. The popular popular American rhythm and blues groups were the Four Tops, the Temptations, the Supremes, the Shirelles, and Martha and the Vandellas. Also popular was Marvin Gaye, Otis Redding, Sam Cooke, Solomon Burke, Wilson Pickett, Mary Wells, Inez Foxx, Gladys Knight, Booker T and the MGs, Johnny Taylor, and Jimmy Reed. These and many more kept everyone dancing and having fun year-round. Most 45 rpm records cost a dollar; an album cost three to five dollars, depending on who made it. A new song would come out about every three months, and the records sold out fast. Everyone had turntables for playing records. The turntables were made so up to five records at a time could be stacked—when one finished, another would be released. We had good soul music.

In early summer 1964, my brother Lester was seeing a young lady with the last name of Hasty who lived at 193 St. James Place, Brooklyn. This would be the prelude to how I would meet my future wife, who would become the mother of our seven children. Both Lester and I worked at Maimonides Hospital, and it just so happened that on one day, we were off work on the same day. I mostly did not go out with Lester; I loved to stay home and read books. But on this day, I was with Lester on St. James Place, and a group of us were just talking and passing time.

A young girl walked by, and of course Lester said something to her; he always did. For some unknown reason, every girl would stop and talk to him. When this girl passed by, I told Lester to leave her alone. He said, "Mind your affairs and leave mine alone." So I said no more. Later, when she walked away, Lester told us her name was Rachael Purifoy. She was up here from Alabama and was living with her sister at 469 Washington Avenue, around the corner. Although I couldn't have known it at that time, Rachael would later become my sister-in-law.

From time to time, Lester would mention her name but I didn't see her again for more than two months. I was getting up early for work every morning and arriving home around 4:30 p.m. I would eat a can of spaghetti and meatballs or a cold-cuts sandwich and go straight to sleep. Sometimes I would wake at one or two in the morning and would just stay up until it was time for me to leave for work. Sometimes I would have a hard time staying awake at that hour, but I was afraid that I would go back to sleep and not wake up on time; that I would not hear the clock. So I got in the habit of doing this.

One morning, this habit caught up with me. I went to sleep right after I came home from work, and I woke up at 2:30 a.m. I said to myself, "I'll sit here on the bed and wait until it's time to leave for work." I put the radio on low and sat down. I had to be at work at 7:00 a.m.

The next thing I knew, I heard children playing outside in the street. I opened my eyes and realized that it was bright and sunny, and cars and trucks were going about the streets. I looked at the clock—it was 3:15 p.m.! I jumped up, going crazy "I was asleep all day!" I said to myself. "How did I do that?" I remember thinking that nobody would believe this. How could I convince anyone that this had happened?

I just knew my job was gone, because I had not called in to say I would not be in. The next day I went to work, just like I always did, but expecting to get fired. But after explaining to my supervisor what had happened, he just looked at me and said, "Claude, go to work." Whew! I was one happy young man.

Then it happened—I met her on August 22, 1964. Mary Aileen Purifoy was one month shy of her eighteenth birthday. Lester had told me his friend Rachael had a sister visiting from Alabama, and he suggested that I come meet her. I really was not interested in a relationship; I had wanted to return home to North Carolina. But Lester would not let up on me and insisted I meet this young lady. One afternoon I went to the house to meet her, but she never came out of her room. Later, she told me she was not feeling well that night. The next time, however, was a sure thing. I was coming home from work about 4:00 p.m.—I was on Tompkins Avenue at Gates Avenue, and Lester drove up to me in a rental car. His friend Rachael was in the front seat with him, and in the backseat was her sister. Lester said, "Come to Coney Island with us."

I did not want to go, so I made up an excuse, saying I had nothing to wear. He said, You can use something of mine." So after changing clothes, we headed to Coney Island Amusement Park. Rachael's sister and I had very little conversation on the way, other than telling each other our name, age, and the school we attended.

Later, we had fun riding the Ferris wheel and a few other rides, but mostly I remember her trying to win a teddy bear from one of the many crooked game stands. A person could spend several dimes and never win because the games were rigged. The only "winner" was someone who pretended to be a regular customer but who was really one of the game attendants. So we did not win a teddy bear. Instead, we had Nathan's franks (a popular hot dog) and a soda.

Mary was very shy. She was not used to eating in front of so many people, so we saved our franks to eat on the way home.

We took Rachael and Mary home at about 11:00 p.m.—that was the time their sister had said for them to be home. From then on, any time I wanted to take Mary out to a movie or to meet my family, I always had to ask her sister Lila first and wait until she gave the okay, even though Mary had finished school and was grown, and I was grown and working full time. But that's part of the respect people had at that time.

The year 1965 was super-good—a complete year of house parties on the weekend, good music, Coney Island, movies, and stores without security gates in front of them. We could window shop all night long on Fulton Street. We could park in front of Macy's; then it was A&S department store. A&S was a very expensive store. I worked at Methodist Hospital in the X-ray department as an escort and also was on the bowling team. My team was known as the Alley Cats. We were a mixed-race bowling team and won first place that year. While working at Methodist Hospital, my coworker and old classmate, George Springs, told me he saw my old friend Wallace Vaughan sleeping by a movie house on Fulton Street in Brooklyn. I told him to send Wallace to see me at the hospital. Wallace later wrote to me when I was in Vietnam. He was always nice to my wife and children. Wallace and I eventually worked together at State Street Garage. We remained friends up until his death in 1990 from the AIDS virus.

Our group of friends included Willie Poe (whom we called "Bo Diddley"), Wallace Vaughn, my brother Lester, James Purifoy and his wife, Margaret Ann, Rachael Purifoy (later to become Rachael McQueen), and Mary Purifoy (later to become Mary McQueen). Rachael and Mary moved out of their sister Lila Mae Blue's apartment to get their own place at 441 Waverly Avenue, between Gates and Greene avenues. This is where they lived in the summer of 1965. In August 1965, New York City had the first blackout. I had a one-room place, top floor rear, at 126 St. Mark's Avenue, near Flatbush Avenue. The night of the blackout, my bowling league was bowling at Caton Bowl in Sunset Park, Brooklyn, when someone came in and said all the street lights were out—and that's when everything went black. One of my coworkers who was on another team had a car, and he said he would take us home.

On New Year's Day 1966, Mary and I came together as one. She became my common law wife, and we both knew we were meant to be together. She would turn twenty years old in '66, and I would turn twenty-one. Mary had a beautiful skin tone, and she used no makeup—she had natural beauty. She had jet-black hair, and her black-rimmed eyeglasses added to the luster she had. She only weighed 118 pounds.

I was a skinny dude—broad shoulders and tight muscles, weighing 129 pounds, soaking wet. When we walked the streets together, we got attention. I was renting a kitchenette room at 126 St. Mark's Avenue at that time, and we said we would start out there. The place where she lived with her sister was not a good place to be at that time, and I wanted her with me. Mary would make great soups, bake chicken, and make rice, beef stew, and sometimes a cake in that one room.

In early summer 1966, I received word that my aunt Annie Bell had died in North Carolina. Mary traveled with me to attend the funeral. She met my mom and sister for the first time. Although it was a sad occasion, we turned the trip into a vacation and had a great time.

Mary and I spent weekends at the movies or sometimes at house parties. Sometimes we just stayed home by ourselves, reading or playing cards together. In August 1966, she and I were invited on an outing to Bear Mountain State Park with my brothers and their families. We had a great time. This was the first for both of us, being high up on a mountain. We were able to see far and wide.

It was soon after that trip to Bear Mountain State Park that Mary told me I was going to be a father. I couldn't believe it! I walked around with my head high, but I also was nervous, as most men are. I was wondering if I could be a strong, supportive father, the way my mother had asked me to be. Could I change the baby's diaper without sticking the baby with the diaper pins? (This was before disposable diapers.) Would I be able to get a job that paid enough to support my wife and baby?

These questions that run through a man's mind when he finds out for the first time that he will soon become a father. I became overly protective in some ways. For example, I did not want Mary to wear pants of any kind—I feared they were too tight around the waist for the baby. I did not want her to eat certain foods, such as barbeque or any spicy foods at all. When we used a car service, I would always warn the driver to take it easy to avoid potholes because my wife was pregnant.

Even with all the precaution, when we had the first snow and ice in early 1967, Mary slipped on the ice and went down. Fortunately, she and baby were not hurt. In fact, we got a good laugh about it later—it seemed we were being careful but not careful enough.

As I've mentioned, we would spend our weekends watching TV—that is, if the TV was not in the pawn shop. Our routine was that we would pawn the TV on Tuesday or Wednesday, take it out on Friday or Saturday after I got paid, watch it over the weekend, and repeat this the next week. We would always watch the Sunday night news to get the Vietnam War report. Newscasters always made the war seem justified. They would report that three to five GIs had been killed and hundreds of Vietcong were killed. I could not understand the huge difference—not until I was directly involved.

My opinion was somewhat 50/50 about the war at that time. In one way, I somewhat wanted to put on the army uniform and look good in front of people—mainly Mary and my family. But the other side of me said it was wrong to be out there, hunting down other humans to hurt them. I was truly unable to get the right view of where I should be. I had no one to help me make the right choice. So I just settled down to await my first-born child. I could not have guessed that very, very soon, I would be in the middle of Vietnam myself. All during this time period, I was dealing with a very bad drinking habit.

On New Year's Day 1967, Mary and I were home at 126 St. Mark's Avenue. This one-bedroom kitchenette did not have its own bathroom—we had to share the bathroom in the hall with another tenant on the floor. We were very quiet because the landlady did not allow women to live with the men renters—she didn't know Mary was living with me. Mary and I wanted to be together because our baby was due to arrive in four months. We hoped the baby would come on my birthday, April 10, but she arrived on April 14.

I was no longer working at Methodist Hospital. The hospital work was good pay every two weeks, and I had been very popular on the job, but I left the job because I owed credit to some cheap credit stores. I could not keep up the payments, and the hospital would not honor garnishes on their workers. So I had a choice of paying off the creditors or leaving the job. I had no money to pay off the debt, so I left the job.

At this time I had forgotten all about the army. Mary and I would watch the news about Vietnam and how many GIs were killed or hurt. I remember thinking, *Boy, I'm glad I failed the written test in 1965 or I would be there.* Little did I know what awaited me in just a few months. In the meantime, however, I was working in a greeting card factory, Charm Craft, at Thirty-Sixth Street and Third Avenue, Brooklyn, for forty dollars a week. Our rent was eighteen dollars a week, which should have given us enough money for other expenses, but I had developed a very bad habit of drinking almost every weekend; I just could not kick the habit. It was getting worse and worse, and my problem with alcohol was creating other problems in my life. It eventually would take me thirty more years—and some major problems with my health and my life—before I got over the desire to drink. I did not know Jehovah God at this time, but today I know he was looking after me, even then.

Mary would go to Cumberland Hospital for her routine checkups, and she would then tell me the updates on the baby. I worked at Charm Craft from 8:00 a.m. until 4:30 p.m., Monday through Friday, as well as some

Saturdays from 8:00 a.m. until noon. Mary would prepare good meals for us. The apartment didn't have a stove, so she used a two-pan hot plate. Sometimes we bought ready-cooked meals, but even though a full-course meal of chicken or pork chops, with all the side orders, was only $1.25 to $1.75, we could not afford to buy a plate every day. We could do that only on weekends. So Mary would cook us homemade soup, or she would fry fish or chicken or whatever she could cook on this little hot plate. Rachael and Lester would come by to eat with us some days, and after we ate, we would always walk them halfway home. That was the routine. If we were at their house, they would walk us halfway home.

By February 1967, we knew we would need to find a place on a lower floor, because it was now too much for Mary to climb the stairs. We were concerned about her falling on the stairs. I found a place around the corner, two blocks away, at 618 Carlton Avenue—a nice, large room with cooking allowed. The landlady lived downstairs. She found out three weeks after we moved in that Mary was expecting a baby and wanted us to move that very day.

I was at work, but when I came home, Mary told me what had happened. The landlady and her son had come to the apartment and had given Mary a hard time. I went down to the landlady's apartment, ready to fight, but they would not open the door for me, and they called the police.

When the cops came, however, the tables turned on the landlady. They told her she had no right to come to the apartment in the first place, and she was only to speak to me because it was my name on the agreement. Also, the cops told her she would have to give us twenty-four hours to leave. We could have stayed until the next day, but I knew it would be trouble. I most surely would have attacked the son that night, if not the landlady, because I did not like the way they'd approached Mary. So I set out again, looking for a place to rent. Right around the corner, in the same block from which we had just moved, I saw a sign in the window: ROOM FOR RENT. I rang the bell, and a lady told me it was twenty-two dollars a week, plus a one-week security deposit. I had exactly forty-four dollars to my name between then and the next payday. I asked her if she had any reservations about my having my pregnant girlfriend with me. She said, "That's not my business; that's your business." So now we had a place to stay, and cooking was permitted.

We continued to wait for the baby's arrival. In those days the parents never knew the baby's gender before birth, so parents did not shop in advance for clothes, as is common today.

My brother Johnnie also lived on the same block at the time, as he also had come up to New York. He and Mary hit it off very nicely; they always joked with each other. They became like brother and sister. She always corrected him when he brought different girls around for her to meet. Mary would tell him to stick with just one friend. Curtiss, Willie Fred, Louis, Betty, and Ida all would come by to see us. Everyone was waiting for the baby. In early April 1967, we started getting false labor. We visited the hospital several times, but the baby was not ready to make her grand appearance. So we continued to wait.

Then, on Thursday night and into early Friday morning, April 14, 1967, we arrived at Cumberland Hospital at North Portland and Auburn Place. Mary was admitted to the maternity ward, and Sheryl was born at 10:03 a.m., weighing six pounds, three ounces. She was the quite baby in the nursery—the nurses told us that she was the "nice one." She had so many visitors that night; everyone was there to see her.

Sheryl came home on a Tuesday, dressed entirely in pink. She took over my side of the bed, and I had to sleep in a chair or on the floor, but I did not mind—we had our baby home. Her name was meant to be spelled with a *C*—Cheryl—but due to a typing error it was spelled "Sheryl," and we did not change it. Sheryl drank Carnation milk mixed with water. In early May 1967, when Sheryl was little over a month old, I received a letter stating that I was to report for induction into the Armed Forces of the United States of America, army branch. It had this warning: THIS IS AN ORDER.

I was shocked out of my mind. I remember saying, "I am being taken away from my wife and baby." When I was ready to volunteer in 1965, I was rejected because of my failure to pass the written test. Now, as the war heated up in Vietnam, the government was ready to accept me. I was very, very angry about this. But also I knew that if I did not report, I could go to jail, and this would make a bad name on my family. I was to report on May 18, 1967, at 7:00 a.m. sharp.

~A CHANGE IS ABOUT TO COME~

I did not want to go to the army, and I was thinking of all kinds of crazy ways to get out of it. I thought about crossing the border to Canada to get out of it, as some guys were doing. But I knew I could never return to the United States without going to jail for desertion, which would not be good. Then I could never get a job anywhere, among the many other things I would lose. So I accepted the fact that I must report and be inducted.

I was to report on a Friday morning. I drank a lot of cheap wine the night before and woke up stinking, but I washed really fast, kissed Mary and Sheryl good-bye, and rode a train and bus to Fort Hamilton army base in Brooklyn, New York, where I was joined by hundreds of other guys, all eighteen to twenty-five years old. I was twenty-two and looked good, with a twenty-nine-inch waist and weighing only 140 pounds.

Guys tried everything to fail the test. Some exchanged urine. Some pricked their fingers and let drops of blood drip into their urine cups to offset the test. Some chewed on bits of soap to fake a seizure. No one wanted to go to war. And then there were those who did want to go, just to shoot other people. And there were those who really thought that they were doing the right thing to fight for their country.

I tried to get out of going by telling the instructor that I was near-sighted and cross-eyed and that I saw double. The instructor just said, "That's all right. You only need one eye to see, so just put a patch over one eye, and you won't see double anymore."

I was inducted at noon and took the pledge to defend the United States. By 5:00 p.m. I was on a bus heading to Grand Central Station in New York City to board a railway train to Columbia, South Carolina, to begin training in jungle warfare. There were five busloads heading the same place.

I could not call Mary and Sheryl; we didn't have a phone in our apartment. So I called my brother Robert Lewis and asked if he could go by the house and let May know what had happened; he said he would.

We boarded a coach train in New York but when we reached Washington DC, they put us in a part of the train that was called a sleeper car—two guys per sleeper, one up top and one below. The train passed right through Southern Pines and Aberdeen, North Carolina, where I'd gone to school. The train only stopped for a couple of minutes to drop off mail and pick up mail, but I saw a few people I knew. We had good food on the train, played cards, told jokes, and slept.

We arrived in Columbia on Saturday afternoon. Army trucks awaited us to bring us to the base. The trouble started once we were on the base. As soon as our feet touched the ground, the veteran drill sergeants started cursing us, yelling at us, and calling us names. They made it very clear they did not like anyone from New York City. They made us double-time run everywhere we went. When we would finish our breakfast, lunch, or dinner, as soon as we came out the door of the mess hall, we had to start running. We could never, ever walk back to our work or sleeping building.

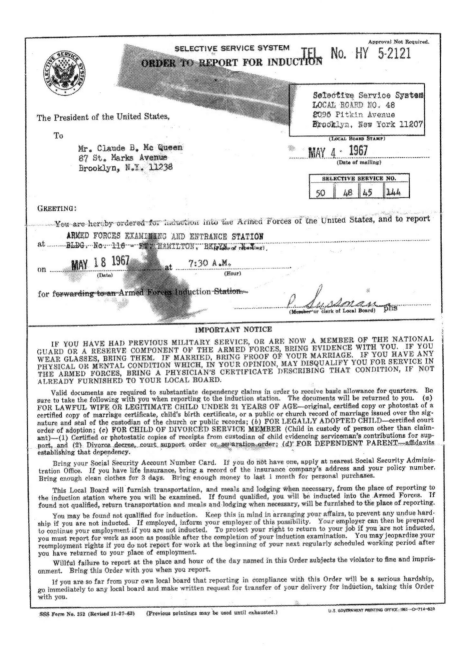

SELECTIVE SERVICE SYSTEM

ORDER TO REPORT FOR INDUCTION

TEL. No. HY 5-2121

Approval Not Required.

The President of the United States,

To

Mr. Claude B. Mc Queen
87 St. Marks Avenue
Brooklyn, N.Y. 11238

Selective Service System
LOCAL BOARD NO. 48
2095 Pitkin Avenue
Brooklyn, New York 11207

(LOCAL BOARD STAMP)

MAY 4 - 1967
(Date of mailing)

SELECTIVE SERVICE NO.			
50	48	45	144

GREETING:

You are hereby ordered for induction into the Armed Forces of the United States, and to report

at ARMED FORCES EXAMINING AND ENTRANCE STATION
BLDG. No. 116 - FT. HAMILTON, BKLYN, N.Y. (Place of reporting).

on MAY 18 1967 at 7:30 A.M.
(Date)   (Hour)

for forwarding to an Armed Forces Induction Station.

P. Sussman
(Member or clerk of Local Board) phs

IMPORTANT NOTICE

IF YOU HAVE HAD PREVIOUS MILITARY SERVICE, OR ARE NOW A MEMBER OF THE NATIONAL GUARD OR A RESERVE COMPONENT OF THE ARMED FORCES, BRING EVIDENCE WITH YOU. IF YOU WEAR GLASSES, BRING THEM. IF MARRIED, BRING PROOF OF YOUR MARRIAGE. IF YOU HAVE ANY PHYSICAL OR MENTAL CONDITION WHICH, IN YOUR OPINION, MAY DISQUALIFY YOU FOR SERVICE IN THE ARMED FORCES, BRING A PHYSICIAN'S CERTIFICATE DESCRIBING THAT CONDITION, IF NOT ALREADY FURNISHED TO YOUR LOCAL BOARD.

Valid documents are required to substantiate dependency claims in order to receive basic allowance for quarters. Be sure to take the following with you when reporting to the induction station. The documents will be returned to you. (a) FOR LAWFUL WIFE OR LEGITIMATE CHILD UNDER 21 YEARS OF AGE—original, certified copy or photostat of a certified copy of marriage certificate, child's birth certificate, or a public or church record of marriage issued under the signature and seal of the custodian of the church or public records; (b) FOR LEGALLY ADOPTED CHILD—certified court order of adoption; (c) FOR CHILD OF DIVORCED SERVICE MEMBER (Child in custody of person other than claimant)—(1) Certified or photostatic copies of receipts from custodian of child evidencing serviceman's contributions for support, and (2) Divorce decree, court support order or separation order; (d) FOR DEPENDENT PARENT—affidavits establishing that dependency.

Bring your Social Security Account Number Card. If you do not have one, apply at nearest Social Security Administration Office. If you have life insurance, bring a record of the insurance company's address and your policy number. Bring enough clean clothes for 3 days. Bring enough money to last 1 month for personal purchases.

This Local Board will furnish transportation, and meals and lodging when necessary, from the place of reporting to the induction station where you will be examined. If found qualified, you will be inducted into the Armed Forces. If found not qualified, return transportation and meals and lodging when necessary, will be furnished to the place of reporting.

You may be found not qualified for induction. Keep this in mind in arranging your affairs, to prevent any undue hardship if you are not inducted. If employed, inform your employer of this possibility. Your employer can then be prepared to continue your employment if you are not inducted. To protect your right to return to your job if you are not inducted, you must report for work as soon as possible after the completion of your induction examination. You may jeopardize your reemployment rights if you do not report for work at the beginning of your next regularly scheduled working period after you have returned to your place of employment.

Willful failure to report at the place and hour of the day named in this Order subjects the violator to fine and imprisonment. Bring this Order with you when you report.

If you are so far from your own local board that reporting in compliance with this Order will be a serious hardship, go immediately to any local board and make written request for transfer of your delivery for induction, taking this Order with you.

SSS Form No. 252 (Revised 11-27-62)   (Previous printings may be used until exhausted.)   U.S. GOVERNMENT PRINTING OFFICE: 1963—O-714-628

1. LAST NAME - FIRST NAME - MIDDLE NAME	2. SERVICE NUMBER	3. SOCIAL SECURITY NUMBER
MC QUEEN, CLAUDE B.	US 62 007 160	

4. DEPARTMENT, COMPONENT AND BRANCH OR CLASS	5a. GRADE, RATE OR RANK	b. PAY GRADE	6. DATE OF RANK	
ARMY RA-US Inf	SP4 (P) (Sic) E-4	E-4	18 Apr 68	

7. PLACE OF BIRTH		8. DATE OF BIRTH	
IX Scotland County, North Carolina		10 Apr 45	

10a. SELECTIVE SERVICE NUMBER	b. SELECTIVE SERVICE LOCAL BOARD NUMBER, CITY, COUNTY, STATE AND ZIP CODE	c. DATE INDUCTED
50 18 45 144	LB # 48, Brooklyn, New York 11207	18 May 67

11a. TYPE OF TRANSFER OR DISCHARGE	b. STATION OR INSTALLATION AT WHICH EFFECTED
Transferred to USAR (See 16)	Fort Hood, Texas

12. REASON AND AUTHORITY	13a. CHARACTER OF SERVICE	b. TYPE OF CERTIFICATE ISSUED	EFFECTIVE DATE
See VI Ch 2 AR 635-200 SPN 201 Expiration of Term of Service Co C 1st Bn 51st Inf 2d Armd Div Fort Hood, Texas FOURTH US ARMY	HONORABLE	None	29 May 69

14. DISTRICT, AREA COMMAND OR CORPS TO WHICH RESERVIST TRANSFERRED	15. REENLISTMENT CODE
Transferred to USAR Control Group(AnlTng) USAAC St Louis MO 63132	RE-1A & 3B

18. GRADE, RATE OR RANK AT TIME OF ENTRY INTO CURRENT ACTIVE SVC.	20. PLACE OF ENTRY
PVT (P) E-1	Brooklyn, New York

13 May 73 NA

21. HOME OF RECORD AT TIME OF ENTRY INTO ACTIVE SERVICE	22. STATEMENT OF SERVICE		YEARS	MONTHS	DAYS
87 St Marks Avenue Brooklyn (Kings) New York 11238	CREDITABLE FOR BASIC PAY PURPOSES	(1) NET SERVICE THIS PERIOD	1	1	28
		(2) OTHER SERVICE	0	0	0
		(3) TOTAL	1	11	28

23a. SPECIALTY NUMBER & TITLE		c. TOTAL ACTIVE SERVICE	1	11	28
11B20 Lt Wpns Infantryman	NA	d. FOREIGN AND/OR SEA SERVICE USARPAC	0	11	24

24. DECORATIONS, MEDALS, BADGES, COMMENDATIONS, CITATIONS AND CAMPAIGN RIBBONS AWARDED OR AUTHORIZED
Vietnam Service Medal w/2 Bronze Service Stars   National Defense Service Medal Republic of Vietnam Campaign Medal   Combat Infantryman Badge Sharpshooter (Rifle)   Expert (M-60 MG)

25. EDUCATION AND TRAINING COMPLETED
Ft Gordon - Lt Wpns Infantry

26a. NON-PAY PERIODS TIME LOST (Preceding)	b. DAYS ACCRUED LEAVE PAID	27a. INSURANCE IN FORCE (NSLI or USGLI)	b. AMOUNT OF ALLOTMENT	MONTH
1 Sep - 14 Sep 67	None (See 30)	YES X NO	NA	NA
	c. VA CLAIM NUMBER	29. SERVICEMEN'S GROUP LIFE INSURANCE		
	NA	X $10,000 $5,000 NONE		

30. REMARKS
3 Years High School   Table 2-3 AR 601-280 applies Blood Group: "O" Item 5a: PFC (P) E-3 Aptd 15 Dec 67 Item 26b: Excess leave of 2 days from 17 Mar 69 thru 18 Mar 69

31. PERMANENT ADDRESS FOR MAILING PURPOSES AFTER TRANSFER OR DISCHARGE	32. SIGNATURE OF PERSON BEING TRANSFERRED OR DISCHARGED
370-A Grand Avenue Brooklyn (Kings) New York 11238	*Claude B. McQueen*

33. TYPED NAME, GRADE AND TITLE OF AUTHORIZING OFFICER	34. SIGNATURE OF OFFICER AUTHORIZED TO SIGN
SANDRA S. DRAPER, 1LT, WAC, Act Asst AG	*Sandra S. Draper*

DD FORM 214

Columbia, South Carolina, was very racist in 1967. All the restaurants and movies were segregated. WHITE ONLY signs were everywhere. Even in army uniform, I could not go in places where white soldiers could go. I was called "boy," "nigger," and "trash," and if the police witnessed this abuse, they would look the other way. I was able to get a three-day pass in June 1967 and used it to come home to New York to see Mary and Sheryl. At this time they had moved in with her sisters Lila Mae and Rachael at 469 Washington Avenue. I was only able to stay with them for two days, but we really enjoyed each other.

Once back on the base, drill sergeants continued to drill and train me in all types of weapons of that time. I would be blasted awake at 4:30 a.m. every day. There were thirty guys in one large room, with fifteen bunks on each side. The sergeant came down the line, blowing his whistle, and we had to be up when he came back up the line. If we were not, he would dump our mattress on the floor. For extra punishment, he would wake us up the following morning at 3:30, and the morning after that, it would be 2:30, until he broke us into obeying orders. We had one hour to shower, shave, and make our bed—military-style tight and neat, so a dime could bounce on it. If the bed was not made this way, the sergeant would pull everything on the floor and tell us to start again.

At 5:30 a.m., we would be on the exercise field. We would be put through every type of exercise and did them all. There was no way to get out of it because the sergeants were watching. Doing push-ups was the number-one workout. We did push-ups all the time. If we forgot an order, such as forgetting to salute an officer, he would stop us in our tracks and order us to give him twenty, thirty, or even a hundred push-ups—it was never fewer than twenty. The morning exercise would end each day with a mile run around the track. Breakfast was between 6:30 and 6:55. At 7:00 a.m., every soldier on every base in the United States will be on the field, in formation, to hear the horn to start the day. We ate lunch in the field and continued training, until everyone returned to formation at 5:00 p.m. to end the day.

In July 1967, my brother Willie came to visit me on base, and he brought Mommy with him. It was a surprise visit that made me feel like a million dollars, just to see someone I knew. We had fun eating and talking.

My basic training finished two weeks later, and the next phase of training started with my orders to report to Fort Benning, Georgia, for advanced infantry training. This training was to get us ready for real combat in the war zone. This training also allowed us to volunteer for Airborne Training, where we would sometimes be dropped from a plane into the heat of a battle or dropped behind enemy lines. I volunteered for this but never knew the reason why.

This training was hard, fast, rough, and only for the extremely fit guys. If someone was weak, lazy, or had no get-up-and-go, he would never survive even two days. But I was doing quite well with the training. The letters I received from home told me that Mary was lonesome for me and missed me. Although she was in a house with her sister, it was not what she wanted.

When I got paid on September 1, 1967, I started drinking beer with the guys and suddenly, I wanted to go home. I told a few guys what I was thinking, and some said I should go, but others said, "You sure you want to go AWOL?" (This meant "absent without leave.") I thought more about it and then said, "Yes, I am leaving tonight. You guys continue without me." I went to the barracks and hurriedly packed a few things in my duffel bag. Then I caught the last bus that left the base that night, rode into town to the Greyhound bus station, paid for a ticket to New York City, and sat down for the long trip.

I arrived in New York on Saturday, September 2 about 7:00 p.m. No one knew I was coming. I rang the bell at Mary's sister's house, and I heard her say, "It's Claude, Mary" before she opened the door. I came inside and found Mary, holding Sheryl, in the kitchen. Sheryl was now three and a half months old and was dressed in her little pink booties. I sat down and held her for a long time. Then Mary and I left to go to Lester and Rachael's house, where we stayed the night. Mary and I talked about many things while I was home, AWOL. I let her know I was going to war and might not return, so I told her I wanted to marry her before I was shipped out. We set the date to marry, but in those days, everyone had to take a blood test before they could marry, and we couldn't afford the fifteen dollars for the test. Also, the wait time for the blood test results was five days, and because I was AWOL, the military police could pick me up at any time, so mostly I stayed inside the house. At that time, if a soldier was AWOL for more than thirty days, he was considered a deserter from the country's forces, and he certainly would go to jail. I left New York on September 8 for Aberdeen to visit with Mommy before returning to my base in Columbia. I knew I would soon be going overseas to war and wanted to see my mother before I left. I spent five days with Mommy in Aberdeen and told her I was AWOL. She understood why I'd come home to see Mary and Sheryl, but now my time was up, and I had to face the wrong I had done.

I brought a Trailways bus ticket for Columbia and arrived in Augusta, Georgia, the next day. I was hungry, broke, and tired, so I wanted to eat before I returned to base, because I did not know for sure what awaited me—jail or hard labor. I had no money, but I did have a nice seventy-dollar Benrus watch with tiny diamonds inside. I loved this watch. I'd bought it on credit when I worked at Methodist Hospital, and I did not want to part with it, but I was hungry. I went into the pawn shop, through the door that read COLORED PEOPLE ONLY, and asked how much I could get on the watch. The clerk looked at it closely and said he could give me eight dollars, and I said I'd take it. Then I asked if I could send money to retrieve the watch and if he would mail it to me if I was shipped out before I could get back to town. He agreed that he would send it to me, but I never saw my nice watch again. (P.S., I never sent money to retrieve it anyway.)

Before I went to base, I bought two hot dogs with mustard and relish. I loved relish and Nehi grape soda. I sat down in the bus station to eat. Then I brought two packs of Viceroy cigarettes and got on the army base shuttle bus to go to the military police barracks to turn myself in. I reported in as being AWOL. They treated me with respect and called my first sergeant from my unit to come over and pick me up. This man was extremely mad at me. He gave me a very hard time. He kept saying, "No trooper goes AWOL on me." He said he would make me pay for going AWOL. He put me on hard extra duty, meaning at 5:00 p.m., when most of the base could relax, my work would be just beginning. I could not go to the PX (the commissary). I could not use any after-hours things, like the pool room, bowling alley, or softball field. I had to clean bathrooms, mop, and shine boots up to 11 o'clock every night. Also he fined me half my monthly pay for three months. I was only being paid ninety dollars per month, so it was cut down to forty-five dollars. Also, I could not make any phone calls at all.

I tried to write to Mary but got in more trouble because the envelopes I used were not to be used for personal mail; they were only for government use. All my letters were put in the garbage, and some had photos in them—photos that were very much cherished. This was the government's way of dealing with me to keep me under the control they wanted.

I finished training in all types of weapons. Our basic weapon was the M-14 rifle, a long, heavy, twenty-bullet magazine. A bayonet knife could be attached on the tip for hand-to-hand combat. Just before I received my orders for Vietnam, we were switched over to the M-16 automatic twenty-clip lightweight rifle to be used in the war.

I had been dropped from the airborne jump class because of my AWOL record. That group of soldiers was now two weeks ahead of me, and I was with another group. In hindsight, this might have helped save my life: later, I found out that the group I should have been in had been shipped up north in Vietnam, and most were killed in an ambush on Christmas Day 1967.

I received my orders in late October 1967. I was to report to Oakland Air Force Base in California on December 1, 1967, to await orders for where I would join a fighting unit for one year in the jungle of Vietnam. The sergeant who told me he would make me pay for going AWOL told me that he hoped I wouldn't make it back home. This same sergeant was killed in a head-on car crash two months after I was sent to Vietnam.

I was allowed twenty-six days leave, starting November 3 and ending the day after Thanksgiving. I was happy at home with Sheryl, who was now six and a half months old, and Mary, now living in a one-room kitchenette on the ground floor, with an inside bathroom and a backyard. We took the blood test as soon as I got home so we could marry before I had to leave. We set Wednesday, November 14, 1967, as our wedding day. I looked around for a preacher to marry us and found one at the municipal building in downtown Brooklyn. He said we would need to come to his house on Hancock Street at 7:00 p.m. My brother Willie Fred and his wife, Ida, would come with us as witnesses, and we would borrow Ida's wedding rings to use.

The wedding rings I had bought for Mary were in the pawn shop. When we needed ten or twenty dollars for food, her rings were all we had to pawn, except for the nineteen-inch black-and-white TV. After the wedding, Fred and Ida brought us back home to Grand Avenue, and we ate our precooked dinner of pork chops, rice, spinach, bread, and Kool-Aid. Sheryl had her bottle and apple sauce, which she really liked.

After a Thanksgiving at home, I left the next day to report to Fort Dix, New Jersey. From there I took my first ever plane trip out of Dover Air Base in Maryland for San Francisco, where a shuttle bus would take me across the famous Golden Gate Bridge down to Oakland Bay. There, I would await orders to take another plane across the Pacific Ocean. It was a twenty-three-hour flight, with stops in Hawaii and Guam, then to Saigon, Vietnam.

At home before I left, I'd promised Mary and all my brothers, my mother, and my sister that I would try to be safe and return home, because

I had not asked to go to Vietnam. I had never heard of this place. I had no problem with the Vietnamese people, and I did not believe in hurting anyone. I did not want to fight a war, but I was under government orders— there seemed to be no way out for me.

Prior to coming to California, I had been given so very many inoculations, and while I waited for orders, I continued to get in-country shots. I do not know, even today, what they were for. I didn't ask questions; I just accepted.

San Francisco Bay in Oakland, California, is so very lovely—a cool place to be at any time of year. It was unlike anywhere I had been in my life. The East Coast is different. Out on the bay in Oakland, I felt relaxed and calm. In New York, I always felt uptight and stressed. I waited two weeks for orders; they came somewhere around December 2, 1967. I would be sent to Long Binh, Vietnam, where I would join Company A, 2nd Battalion, 47th Infantry. It was a strong, mechanized unit, fighting in the Mekong Delta rice paddies. I did not like this at all—I had heard about the Delta, and I knew I did not want to be there.

I was out of my mind, trying to find a way out of this mess I was in. Where could I turn? How could I get out? I had no way out; I was in this man's army. I started drinking very heavily, and as the day for me to depart got closer, I drank even more. I was hoping to get drunk charges brought up on me so I could win more time in the United States, but my commanders did not pay any attention to my trick. My plane, with more than three hundred other soldiers, was set to leave San Francisco at 10:00 p.m. on Monday. That day, I drank beer, whiskey, and wine, trying to numb my mind as to what was facing me. But that did not help; it only made me very sick. I boarded a TWA plane with everyone else and remember saying, "Well, this is it." I wrote Mary and Sheryl from the plane, and the stewardess said she would mail the letter for free. All mail from Vietnam was free.

WHY DIE FOR A LOST CAUSE?

What do ATTLEBORO and JUNCTION CITY Operations' failures mean ?

THAT MEAN :

U.S troops with all kinds of modern weapons, whatever their number, will be defeated by the South Vietnam Liberation armed forces in this **ASIAN LAND WAR** !

IT'S OUR AFFIRMATION !

IT'S ALSO THE OPINION OF ONE OF YOUR MOST RENOWNED GENERAL !

● OPPOSE TO YOUR BEING SENT TO THE BATTLEFRONT !
● DEMAND IMMEDIATE REPATRIATION !
● LET THE VIETNAMESE PEOPLE SETTLE THEMSELVES THEIR OWN AFFAIRS !

Tại sao chịu chết cho 1 sự nghiệp chắc chắn sẽ thất bại !

Những thất bại của các cuộc hành quân ATTLEBORO và JUNCTION CITY có ý nghĩa như thế nào ?

ĐIỀU ĐÓ CÓ NGHĨA LÀ :

Quân Mỹ, với đủ mọi loại vũ khí tối tân, dù nhiều đến thế nào, cũng sẽ bị các lực lượng võ trang giải phóng miền Nam Việt-nam đánh bại trong cuộc chiến tranh trên LỤC ĐỊA CHÂU Á NÀY.

ĐÓ LÀ ĐIỀU MÀ CHÚNG TÔI KHẲNG ĐỊNH !

ĐÓ CŨNG LÀ Ý KIẾN CỦA 1 TRONG NHỮNG TƯỚNG LÃNH CÓ TIẾNG TẦM NHỨT CỦA CÁC ANH !

★ PHẢN ĐỐI KHÔNG CHỊU RA CHIẾN TRẬN !
★ HÃY ĐÒI ĐƯỢC HỒI HƯƠNG NGAY !
★ HÃY ĐỂ NHÂN DÂN VIỆT-NAM TỰ GIẢI QUYẾT LẤY CÔNG VIỆC NỘI BỘ CỦA HỌ !

In January 1968, I was in Vietnam. The temperature every day was 90 degrees to 105 degrees. We had a mandatory intake of one salt tablet daily, as well as an anti-malaria pill. Dress code was full combat gear that included a flak vest, which was able to slow down a .45 caliber bullet, if not stop it—if a man was hit, though, it would still knock him off his feet. We also used steel-toed boots because of the many booby traps we faced every time we went out on patrol, and we were never without our helmets. My unit used small tanks to get from one location to another. Then we would patrol on foot. My job most often was as right-flank rifleman. I carried four grenades, two smoke bombs, six to eight ammo pouches, two strings of .60 caliber machine gun ammo, one combat knife, earplugs, a poncho for the rain, anti-mosquito spray, a flashlight, and sometimes a .45 caliber pistol to use when entering dark tunnels. I also carried two or three days' worth of cigarettes and matches, two days' worth of food rations in ready-to-eat military packages, two canteens of water, and candy bars to get quick energy. My personal weapon was a .16 caliber automatic rifle.

Our sector kept us in deep jungle or rubber plantations. We never knew who we were fighting. The farmer we saw by day sometimes would be the one who ambushed us by night. Or the little kid who looked so cute and sweet would walk up to us and drop a live grenade. We learned quickly to be very much on guard.

The country of Vietnam is a great place, very lovely. The people are nice and friendly, but I don't think that most of them wanted us there. They only wanted what the United States could give them at the moment—jobs, schools, and hospitals. What they really wanted was one Vietnam, not a South and North Vietnam, but that's just what they got in 1975, after

65,000 of our soldiers were killed and 200,000 were wounded. What for? *I have yet to understand why we were there.*

By the middle of January 1968, I had already been in three battles. Little did I know, however, what was in front of me. Things started quieting down. We could not find the ones we were fighting. Here and there, we would have a skirmish but nothing heavy or long term. But on January 31, 1968, all the quietness changed. That day was Tet, the Vietnamese New Year. The Tet Offensive was by far the largest battle fought in Vietnam. Why?

1. It caught the United States off guard.
2. It was countrywide.
3. It was city as well as jungle fighting.
4. There was no let-up for four months or more.

It caught my unit by surprise. Remember that this was a very big holiday for the Vietnamese people. Therefore, the United States allowed a truce to go into effect for a total of three days. All sides were to stop fighting, allowing the Vietnamese the right to enjoy themselves. We had been told that there was a lot of enemy movement in the mountains and along the Mekong River, but our government chose to just ignore it.

Our unit was ordered to retreat into a rubber plantation that overlooked a highway (Highway No. 1) that ran from deep in South Vietnam, all the way up north in North Vietnam. We could see crowds of people as they traveled along the highway, going about their daily lives, without bullets and rockets flying everywhere. Then it happened at 2:30 a.m. on January 31, 1968. We got orders to report to the east side of Tan Son Nhut Airport because snipers were shooting at planes. As we moved through the darkness toward the airport, soldiers started falling off our vehicles. At first, we thought it was just an accident, but we quickly found out we had been tricked into an ambush and were under fire. We lost ten men before we could pull back to regroup. As soon as daylight came, we could see what we were up against, and our radio told us we were under a countrywide offensive—this became known as the Tet Offensive.

My unit was trapped because the closest unit that could help us was also under fire. We were pinned down most of that day, unable to move back or forward. The enemy was trying to overrun the airport and blow up as many planes as they could. It was a tough fight because the enemy had dug in very tight, and we had a hard time spotting their many locations. As darkness started to fall, we knew we had to make a move or be overrun. So we called in the gun ships to help us.

But now we faced another problem. We were so close to the enemy that the door gunners on the helicopters could not fire, for fear of hitting their own men. But late that night, another unit was able to fight their way in to our location and together, we were able to hold our own. We fought, nonstop, until February 13, 1968.

The monsoon rain in Vietnam was a sight to see—there is no other rain like it. The weather could be clear, hot, or sunny, and out of nowhere, the rain would start. It rained on and off for six months straight. At times, it was hard rain and so heavy, it seemed to be raining sideways. But this did not stop the fighting or even slow it down. Although we didn't stop fighting, sometimes we would have what was known as "stand-down time." This meant that we, as a company, would return to our base camp for two to three days to completely resupply ourselves and send our loved ones back home special things of the country. We would write letters, get a good shower, clean the inside of our boots, and clean our weapons—this was a necessity so they would work properly. We would also drink beer, play cards, smoke weed, drink liquor, or just relax. We also waited for orders to return to the jungle.

Our shower system was homemade, consisting of a burlap sack that could hold water. We would fill this up with water from a hose while the shower tip was clamped off. Once filled, we would release the clamp and shower fast. All this was done outside in the sun. We truly felt good afterward, but we knew it would be soon back to the field—and personally, we all knew this shower could be our last.

During one such stand-down, I was drinking liquor and beer with some of the guys when someone asked me to try some "weed." I had never in my life done this. I was always a drinker of hard liquor or beer, but with all the guys standing around, I did not want to be the odd man out, so I said okay. I didn't know how to even puff it. I noticed the guy who gave it to me was smearing some wet stuff along the side of the "weed stick" and then told me to puff it. Later, I found out this wet stuff was LSD.

The LSD mixed with the weed was not good for me at all. It affected me in a very, very bad way. It made me go into a laughing spell that I could not control, and it seemed as though everyone standing around me suddenly had turned into horses. I remember saying to them, "Hey, guys, you all look like horses." At that, they all knew I was in trouble. All of them kept telling me to drink as much water as I could, and they walked me around for a long time until I started coming out of it. Keep in mind that I was armed with an automatic M-16 and carrying live hand grenades with me at this time. It could have affected me in a dangerous way, where I could have turned on my own men. I never, *ever* tried that again.

I would receive two or three letters from home every week. Mary would tell me how everyone was, and she also would let Sheryl scribble little scratches on the letters. I really loved to see this. I also would get letters from my brothers and my mom, and a member of the church I joined before coming to Vietnam would write and send newspaper clips of current events. But most important of all, Mary told me that we were now expecting another little one. We both wanted a boy so my name could be carried on. We both prayed that we would have a boy.

There were some nights when my unit would be set up on ambush patrol, and the enemy would be so very close to us. They would sometimes taunt us through their homemade speakers in their broken English. They would try to scare us into giving up our location in the dark of night. They would say things like, "GI, you die tonight" or "GI, you sleep? GI, you sleep?" They would repeat this over and over, hoping we would make the mistake of firing our weapons so they could see the flash and know where to return fire. But we were trained to hold fire under these tricks and just wait until the right time. Also, every night we were in the jungle on ambush or patrol, we would always have our position with what was known as LPs. This meant we had two to four soldiers east, west, north, and south, out about twenty-five yards from our main unit. Their job was to give the main unit advance notice that enemy troops were nearby. They were not to make contact with the enemy but to pull back as soon as the enemy was spotted.

In daylight hours when on patrol, we could always tell if the enemy was around by watching the birds or monkeys. If birds were not flying around in the trees or if the monkeys were making lots of noise, that meant we were walking into an ambush. We knew to be on the lookout and get ready because some action would surely take place.

The Vietcong were not stupid; these guys were well trained, and some were more educated than we were. They had done their research on the ways and means of the American soldiers. For example, they knew that Americans always got lazy and sleepy after breakfast, lunch, or dinner. They also knew that Americans loved to sleep in the early morning hours, between 3:00 a.m. and 6:00 a.m., so they would attack our position at this time. This way they hoped to catch us in a weakened state of mind.

Sometimes they would send out spy girls. They knew most of the American soldiers were eighteen- to twenty-five-year-olds and that they were a long way from home and their wives and girlfriends. The sight of young girls would entice them. The main reason for the girls being there would be to scope out our position—to see how many soldiers were present, what type of weapons we had, and what would be the easy spot to get inside our position. Sometime the enemy would set booby-trap bushes with poison spiders or scorpions ready to sting or bite us as we cleared away the bushes.

The only protection was to always be on guard, stay alert, and trust your fellow trooper. Out in the jungle we did not have a race problem. Everyone needed each other. Also, we had other countries fighting alongside us, so we had to be friendly with them as well. We had forces from New Zealand, South Korea, Thailand, Argentina, and a few more countries joining up with us but fighting separately.

The weather in the jungle ranged from hot to cool. Some days, the ceiling was so very thick that we could not see the sky clearly. The jungle had all types of poisonous snakes, spiders, and ants—all types of bugs. There also were lovely birds that were so colorful.

If a soldier was hurt or killed while fighting, we would carry him on a stretcher to a spot where the helicopter could come down to take out the injured or dead. Sometimes we would need to cut out a spot for the helicopter to land. We called this an "LZ"—landing zone.

Sometimes these LZs could become dangerous, because the Vietcong would wait until the helicopter came in and then fire on it from three or four directions. Sometimes when we were on patrol in the jungle, we suddenly would come upon a body of water—it was right there, deep in the jungle, flowing so quietly that we didn't know it was there until we were right on it. When we needed to cross it, however, I would get nervous. Even though we used rope to support our crossing, I still would panic. This started after seeing a schoolmate almost drown one day when we were playing hooky from school and went swimming. This upset me so that after that, I had a problem with getting in large body of water, even pools.

By mid-March 1968, the fighting had slowed down somewhat so we could at least get baths here and there. We didn't have hot water but the weather was always hot, even when it rained. We used makeshift showers outdoors that worked just fine.

One engagement that I will never forget was when we were sent to a mountain that we called Hill 108. Duncan James, a twenty-year-old white soldier from Tennessee, was a good guy, and we became friends fast. When we got the order to go up Hill 108 to blow up some enemy tunnels, we thought nothing of it. It seemed like a routine assignment; but again, little did I know what we were in for.

We were airlifted to the site by helicopters. In total, we had four squads, each with seven soldiers, one captain, two radiomen, two medics, and two lieutenants—a total of thirty-five men. When we left the next day, there were only seventeen of us—five had been killed in action; thirteen were wounded. My friend James was one of the five killed. This is war. There was nothing nice about it. Things happened—and happened fast, without forewarning sometimes.

We received news that Martin Luther King Jr. was killed, but there were no problems between the black and white soldiers. We all were too busy trying to stay alive. On a personal level, I had expected that Martin would be assassinated, because so many people wanted him out of the way. It was sad that this had happened, but shortly afterward, Robert Kennedy was also killed. Still, the war continued without let-up. I continued to try to stay strong, and Mary kept me updated on Sheryl's progress—how she was growing and progressing. She said our new baby would be born in July.

I was hurt in late April 1968 but not bad enough to return to the United States. Instead, I was given temporary orders with the 716th Military Police to back them up in Saigon. This was a little different; it called for carrying out security in and around the buildings that the US Army used in Saigon for offices or sleeping quarters for those who were not directly involved in the field fighting. I really liked this assignment; it gave me some breathing time—I could relax a little because my duties were not so intense. I really hadn't wanted to leave all the guys in the field, but an order was an order. I had not wanted to fight in the first place—I didn't know these people, and they didn't know me.

Saigon is a beautiful city, and the people were very friendly. They served great vegetables in the restaurants, and we could get the very best noodles or frog, snake, worms, alligator, buffalo, monkey, and other meat. But the main course would always be rice and fish; many types of fish swim in the waters of Vietnam.

During my tour in Vietnam, I never saw American money. We used paper military money, called military payment certificates, or MPCs. So ten cents, five cents, twenty-five cents, and fifty cents all were in paper form. And one dollar of our MPCs was worth two Vietnamese dollars. The Vietnamese were eager to give us two dollars for one of our MCP dollars. MPCs came in different colors—a red bill was twenty dollars, a yellow bill was ten dollars, a blue bill was five dollars, and so forth. The Vietnam black market was loaded with our military money, which they got from prostitutes selling their bodies to army men.

There was a law that forbade them from having this money, but they stashed money everywhere but the bank. So the American military came up with a way to make this stop. All army, navy, air force, marines, and civilians were warned in advance to keep no more than a hundred dollars on their person at any time. We were not to keep money in our lockers on base or anywhere. They gave no reason for the order, but in June 1968, all Americans found out. Overnight, the color of money changed. Whoever had more than a hundred dollars of the old-color money just had to burn it, rip it, or cut it and throw it in the air. It was no longer good for anything. Quite a few Americans lost thousands and thousands of dollars, and no excuse they gave could change the government's stand. It was worthless to try.

But Vietnamese people who had stuffed all that money away began to kill themselves when they found out it was useless. They were crying all over the country. We even found bags of old-color money when we were out on patrol; people just left it.

August 1, 1968, was a great day of joy for me and for my entire company. I had been telling everyone how much I wanted the baby to be a boy, and everyone was rooting for me. I wasn't sure whether or not I would make it back home, and like most men, I wanted a son. I will never forget the moment I was called into the sandbag bunker to hear a message coming across the ham radio airwaves. The message went like this:

ATTENTION!
MIKE CHARLIE slice slice QUEBEC UNION
EHCO ECHO November
Yellow October Union Roger
W H Apple Bravo Bravo
Apple I S WELIMA L

The message was in code; each letter of the alphabet was associated with a certain military word; we learned this early in our training. So the message actually said: "Attention McQueen. Your wife had a baby boy. All is well."

71

I would not see my son for five more months, but I was so very happy—overjoyed—and the company was happy for me. But I still was not home. I had a little girl that I had to leave when she was only one month old. Now I had a son I couldn't see or hold. Mary sent me pictures of Sheryl and Claude—the new baby—and I cherished them. They stayed with me all the time. My orders to return home would not come until November 25, 1968. I had to stay alive in a war zone because I had to see my wife and kids. Only God knows what I had to do to try to make this happen; I had some close calls. But one day I said to myself, *I have only one week left on my tour in Vietnam.* All that week I was careful with everything. I watched what I drank and ate and made sure not to make enemies with anyone. I did not want anything to stop me from getting out of Vietnam.

On the day before I was to leave, I got hugs and well wishes from everyone. But then my nerves went to pieces on me. I did not want to take a twenty-three-and-a-half-hour flight back to the States. I don't know why, but I just couldn't get my nerves up to board the plane. I even asked about coming home by boat and was told I could do that, but it would take one month to cross the Pacific Ocean, and that would not give me any leave time to see my family. Also, the boat would not come to New York but to California. So I said, "Okay, I'll go by plane."

I boarded a huge, ugly Seaboard Airlines plane. The first stop was twelve hours away in Okinawa, Japan. The other guys on the flight and I had a good time playing cards, telling jokes, exchanging addresses, and saying our good-byes. After twenty-three and a half hours in the air, we touched down in San Francisco, back where I started one year ago. I hadn't known how to pray to God at that time, but I learned how to do it now.

~HOMEWARD BOUND~

It was Monday afternoon, a clear, warm day. Everyone got off the plane and rushed to call their homes. I called Brooklyn to let Mary and the kids know I was safely in the States. I could hear Sheryl trying to talk to her mommy. Mary put the phone to Sheryl's ear, but she would not say anything to me. Claude Jr. was four months old now.

As we were clearing customs, I made my mind up that I was not going back in the air. I would go to New York by Greyhound bus.

As soon as we finished going through customs, we were free to leave for our home state. Guys were buying plane tickets to every state. Two guys who were going someplace local asked a cab driver to take them to the bus station. I got in the cab also. The driver asked all of us where we were going. The other guys named a nearby town, but when I said New York, the driver quickly slammed on his brakes. He turned and looked at me and said, "Are you crazy? You want to take a bus cross-country to New York? That will take five days. What's the matter? Don't you have money for a plane ticket? The army will buy you a plane ticket. Did you know a bus just went off the mountain in Utah?"

I told him that yes, I had money, but I just didn't want to fly anymore. I would take my chances by bus.

I got to the Greyhound bus depot in San Francisco around 10:00 p.m. The ticket agent told me that the next cross-country straight-through bus would leave at 8:00 a.m. the next day, Tuesday. I think I read every paper, every book, and every map in the station to stay awake so I wouldn't miss the bus in the morning. I called Mary to let her know what I was doing. She wanted me home fast but she understood and did not press me to change my mind and take a plane. I loved her for that. The next morning, I boarded a Greyhound bus for New York City. I went to the very back so I could lie down, and right away, I went fast to sleep.

I was in military uniform, looking good with ribbons and medals. I put my money under my T-shirt next to my skin, so I would not get robbed. Here I was, going cross-country to New York City. I was told we would arrive in New York City about 1:00 p.m. on Friday. All day Tuesday we crossed California. Las Vegas was next; there were so many oil rigs in Las Vegas that I almost got dizzy. It was exciting, seeing things I'd never seen before. Then came Utah, a short state to cross; then Nebraska; then came Iowa. Next came Missouri, with the Ozark Mountains. I was so high up at one point, I thought my head would explode from the altitude. Also, it was daytime, and I remember seeing the Gateway Arch in St. Louis from at least five miles away. When we reached the Greyhound bus station in St. Louis, I was so sick, I could not continue. I thought I would need to go to a hospital. But after taking over-the-counter headache pills, I felt like I could make it.

During the trip I didn't see any black people until I reached Chicago. I was very nervous about getting off the bus in the little towns out West, being that I was the only black on the bus, and I didn't see any when we would come in to a bus station. Here's what I did to get food:

There was a lady who got on in Las Vegas who had three little kids traveling with her to her mother's in St. Louis. She was leaving her husband. I made friends with the children and when we came in to a station, I told her I would watch the kids if she would buy a frank and soda or chips or candy for me. Of course, I gave her the money for everything I wanted, but she never knew why I did not want to leave the bus. I had no trouble—until I reached Chicago.

When I was in Chicago, a black guy who was buying a ticket to New York wanted to show me around the streets of Chicago before the bus pulled out. I told him that I was not born yesterday, and he would do himself good to stay far away from me, all the way to New York. I knew he was trying to set me up, and I kept one eye on him from then on. I was well built and had fought hand-to-hand combat, so I knew I could take care of myself, one on one.

We crossed West Virginia, New Jersey, and on into New York City. As we pulled into the Port Authority Bus Terminal in New York City—the place I'd left one year ago—I could see my wife, Mary, waiting for me. She was holding my son, Claude Jr., and my niece Inez was holding Sheryl. My brother Willie Fred was also there.

I came off the bus and into the station and kissed my wife for the first time in a year. Sheryl let me pick her up, but Claude Jr. would not let me touch him. I was happy to see my brother and niece there to welcome me home, but New York did not look the same as when I'd left.

Mary, Claude Jr., Sheryl, and I were together as a family for the very first time. Everyone came to the house to see me and ask about Vietnam. At the time, we lived at 370-A Grand Avenue in the basement rear apartment, between Greene and Gates Avenue.

While I was home on leave for thirty days, we visited my mother in Aberdeen, North Carolina, for one week. This is when Claude Jr. became more used to me, because on the bus trip, eleven hours each way, I had to hold either him or Sheryl.

The one thing I remember about Claude Jr. as a baby is that he was really a good baby. He never cried much, and he was always smiling. Oh, how he loved music. One song in particular did something to Junior— "Proud Mary" by Creedence Clearwater Revival. Every time that song came on the radio, he would pop up in his crib, hold the side of his crib, and dance away. Mary and I thought this was so cute. We spent Christmas 1968 in North Carolina.

Early in January 1969, I had to report to my last duty base. I was ordered to Fort Hood, Texas, outside Waco and not far from Dallas.

My mode of transportation again would be two and a half days on a Greyhound bus. I did not want to leave my wife and kids again, but I was under government orders, and the choice was to obey them or go to jail. I packed my duffel bag, kissed everyone good-bye, and off I went.

At Fort Hood, I was assigned to a tank unit. The main job of the tank unit was training guys who were to go over to Vietnam. We were out in the field most of the time, high in the mountains. I only had six months left to serve, until June 29, 1969.

Texas was nice, but it was very cold up in the mountains. At night, once we were in a sleeping bag, boots, jacket, gloves, and wool hat, we did not move, not even if we thought a snake was crawling over us. We did a lot of intense combat training, night and day, but every time we would go out, I would get severe headaches. I went to the doctor, but he could not find anything in the blood tests or X-rays. It was in late April when one of my fellow soldiers told me I was suffering from high-altitude sickness. Each time I would go high in the mountains, I would get sick with headaches. What kept me going was that now I could talk to my wife and kids at least once a week. And Mary and I exchanged well over a thousand letters and cards during the time I served in the army.

When I left New York for Texas that morning, Mary and I were having breakfast at the table, and the kids were asleep. We were listening to the radio, and the weather report said we could get a lot of snow by the weekend—this was a Wednesday morning. Mary and I said we should get a few things in the house, just in case it did snow a lot; then she would not need to go out.

It's good that we did. She went out and I stayed with the kids—and I still made the bus on time. But after I arrived in Texas, that very weekend a big snowstorm hit New York and shut everything down. We were so happy we'd used our heads, and she had things in the house. She told me that she and the kids were inside for a little over one week, unable to get out because of the large banks of snow.

One day in April 1969, I made Soldier of the Day in my company. The company sergeant would select a soldier to be Soldier of the Day at roll call, after inspection, based on the soldier's ability to meet the standard uniform requirement—spit-shined shoes or boots and crisp uniform, as well as locker arrangement and bed arrangement. Everything a solider owned had to be in a certain spot—toothbrush, toothpaste, comb, hairbrush, socks neatly rolled, uniforms neatly hung and all facing the same direction. Bed sheets had to be tight enough to make a dime bounce on the bed. There could not be any paper, books, cups, or other materials visible in the area. The Soldier of the Day had to have excellent posture, too. His reward for being selected was one carton of cigarettes, one cigarette lighter, and a full-day pass to do as he wished—anything other than going to bed.

I remember that I was happy about winning Soldier of the Day, but I could not enjoy it. I just wanted to be home.

War is evil, and Satan the devil directs the movement of war. Here you have human beings who have never met one another, going head to head, toe to toe, and the aim is to kill. Members of each side were put through hardships to get this done. We went for hours without sleep and for days without changing our clothes. We were bitten by all types of bugs and unable to slap or fan them away for fear of making our position known to the enemy. We were told by those who were not combatants to get out of their country and go home where we belonged.

We were unable to go on sick call, even if we were running a fever. We were told these people were our enemies, when we never knew these people before coming here. We'd go to sleep, not knowing when the enemy would strike or if this might be our last battle.

If it was daytime, we might look up to the sky, and it would be blue and beautiful, quiet and peaceful-looking. If it was night and the moon was out, we'd see the stars of heaven maintain their assigned position. All this would make a sane person think and ask the question, "Why are we fighting?"

There is a saying, "All is fair in love and war." Because of the things that took place in this war, we came to believe that statement. For example, the Vietcong had some good ploys to achieve their goal. Two that got our attention was their sending out young girls near our camps or outposts. They knew the young soldiers would get the urge to visit the girls and let their guard down. The soldier would feel safe because he would not see a weapon in the girl's hand, but a few young men never made it home because of their being so trusting.

Here's how this worked:

The girls implanted razors in their vaginas, and when the soldier would attempt sexual intercourse with the girl, he would rip himself. The Vietcong hoped he would bleed to death before help could arrive. The commander of the Vietcong knew it would also kill the girl, but the girl had agreed to go along with this to help her family—her family would now be given food and other needs for a period of time.

Another way was that the Vietcong would kidnap young boys and chain or tie them to a tree. They would place a weapon with one clip of ammo in their hands and just leave them there, telling them to aim carefully at any American troops coming near, and afterward, they should be ready to die. These were school-age boys. This was war, and all is fair in love and war.

At the same time that the war was hot in the deep jungle, the cities were flourishing and partying. The bars would be full at night, with people going about their normal lives as if no war was being fought. The Vietnamese college crowd would not speak to Americans; but every day, planeloads of them would leave for America to continue their studies in medical, law, science, or other subjects.

When we searched a dead Vietcong's body one day, we found a letter from his son and learned that the son was a student at a high-profile school in Brooklyn. I could not believe I was standing over someone who had been shooting at us and at the same time, he had a son educated in Brooklyn, New York. *War is evil.* All is fair in love and war.

I constantly asked myself why I was in Vietnam. I had not asked to be here. How could I get out of here? These questions ran through my mind daily. I felt myself going insane but didn't want to break down in a country so far from home. So I prayed hard to maintain my sanity. I thought of my loved ones. I drank beer. I'd see my buddy losing it as well and somehow know how to give him support. This was not a party. War is evil.

When patrolling through a village and looking at the sadness in children's eyes, we felt compassion for them. We were heavily armed, driving tanks and helicopters overhead, and a little boy or girl would look at us, frightened to death. What did we do in cases like this? Because the kids were too young to understand that we were not there to hurt them, we always carried boxes of candy in the tanks to give out, to try to reassure them—or at least calm them.

War is evil, and no one benefits from it. When we were out on patrol in deep jungle, sometimes we ran out of drinking water. It was 95 to 105 degrees in the jungle, and sometimes we would come upon a body of water. We were thirsty, but did we drink it? No, we didn't. This water was stagnant and not safe to drink. We knew we could get diarrhea or other ailments if we drank it. We would just wash our heads to cool down and hope the resupply helicopter came quickly with drinking water.

I'd look high in the sky and see the shiny jet known as the "Freedom Bird," and I'd feel good and sad at the same time. I'd be glad to know someone was on his way home but sad that so many were left behind. I'd look again and there would be another Vietcong being pushed from an open door of a gunship helicopter, because he would not give up the information needed to find the larger group of Vietcong. Maybe he did not know; maybe he did know. Whatever the case, war is evil.

The people of Vietnam, in general, are kind, peaceful people who mind their own affairs. This war did an injustice to them, as it did to the whole world. I had more than a few conversations with farmers in the fields who would tell of complete destruction of their rice crops and how it hurt their families—it took away the entire year's food supply. Many also spoke of the Agent Orange defoliant that killed the vegetable gardens along with destroying people's lungs. Even today, Vietnam veterans suffer the ill effects of Agent Orange. My wife had a miscarriage in 1972 that we think was directly related to this chemical.

Soon after being discharged from the United States Army, I began to notice I was not well. I became strongly sick, but my sickness was not visible to anyone. My wife would tell me, "Claude, you don't look sick." But I felt real sick. I had headaches that would come on suddenly. Also, my body would feel like it was on fire. I had night sweats, like someone had poured a bucket of water all over me. Foot and body rashes would appear without explanation. I was thirsty all the time. I had nightmares to the point that I did not want to go to sleep sometimes.

I was buying over-the-counter medication that never helped. I visited the Veterans Health Center often. The doctors would order full lab, X-ray, stool and stress test, but all would come back negative. The only thing that seemed to help a little was when I would drink. But then I found that I was only adding to my problem, because I would be very sick for three or four days after I would stop drinking.

I never could understand why the Veterans Health Center could not find what was wrong with me. I wondered if they really knew but did not want to tell. I wondered if it had something to do with all the shots I received before and during my time in Vietnam. I didn't know for sure what I was given. What I did know, however, was that I was a nervous wreck. I was admitted to the Montrose Veteran Hospital, sometimes for weeks at a time, for no other problem than a nervous condition. And this was a large hospital, filled with young men who were unable to function on their own. We all were there for help in readjusting to normal life. It's sad to say, but very few were able to readjust to normal life after a tour in the jungle of Vietnam.

A doctor can help but only so far. He can give medication, fix broken limbs, and watch vital signs, but he cannot give the person peace of mind. We needed help from above. Today, in 2011, I talk to many Vietnam veterans, and everyone has the same voice. They all say, "One—that war messed me up. Two—I'm not the same as I was before I left. Three—I have been sick for years."

Now you tell me if war is not evil.

In May 1969 Mary sent me an application form for public housing. I remember asking myself how I could get in public housing when I got out when I had no job. But I found out that every member of the armed forces who needed housing was given first choice of the open apartments. In other words, our apartment would be waiting for us as soon as I was discharged. That was a blessing at that time. One week after my discharge, we had a choice of three projects: Coney Island, Marcy, or Walt Whitman. We talked it over and selected Walt Whitman. Looking back over the years, I think we made the right choice.

Our rent was based on what I would get from the unemployment insurance, which was $48.00 dollars a week. We had two bedrooms, which was a first for us. Ever since I'd come to New York in 1962, I'd always lived in a one bedroom; the same with Mary. It was difficult for Sheryl because she now would have a wall separating her from Mommy, and we did not want this. So Claude Jr.'s baby bed was with me in one room, and Mary and Sheryl were in twin beds in the other room. But it did not take long before Sheryl and Claude Jr. had the room together.

I was sick at this time with a nervous condition and did not know how sick I was. My major problem was that my nerves seemed all torn up. I could not ride in cars for thinking that the enemy was on the rooftops of buildings or poking guns out windows. I could not tolerate loud noise. Firecrackers were the worst. I was given medication at the VA hospital but soon found out that the problem was made worse. The stuff was very addictive, and I did not want that. I started drinking heavily, because the flashbacks of the war were hard to deal with.

I went for a job interview two weeks after army discharge, and the interview person said she'd never seen a person come for a job so soon after getting out of the service. She said men waited six months to a year or at least until their unemployment checks stopped. I remember telling her that I needed to work because I had a family to take care of. She was very impressed by my statement. She said she had two lazy brothers and a lazy husband, and she was going to tell them about my example of being a man. Sometime later, one of her brothers got a job at the same place I was working, and because I had on army clothes, he asked me which employment office I had used. When I told him, he said his sister had come home and told him about me, and it made him and her husband ashamed, so they both got jobs. He said his brother was looking for work, too. All I could say was "Sometimes you have to be a man."

One Saturday morning in summer 1969, there was a knock on our door that would change our lives. A Jehovah's Witness couple was going door-to-door, encouraging people to read the Bible. I had seen these people in the streets but never talked to them. But this day, here they were at my door. I have always been friendly to everyone I meet, and this was true in this case. I found out they were a married couple named Aaron and Betty Swan. I enjoyed what I heard from them and agreed to a Bible study. Aaron said he would come on Saturdays.

Another person would study with Mary. Her name was Mary Watts. I first studied from a Bible aide book called the *Truth Book*. Although this book is currently out of print and circulation, any Jehovah's Witness who studied the Bible in the late 1960s or early '70s could answer questions about this book—it's truthful and powerful, and even those who know about God our Creator will learn more about him from this book, such as his purpose for the earth.

In August 1969, Claude Jr. was one year old, and it was time for his first haircut. We wondered how he would take it. Would he cry? I went to Ray's Barber Shop on Myrtle Avenue near Fort Greene Park. (The shop is still in operation today, run by the son of the barber who cut Claude

Jr.'s hair. I am an honored guest there and have not paid for a haircut in five years.) Claude Jr. looked a little confused, as if he wondered where his hair was going and why I let the man cut his hair. But when I got in the chair and held him and got my hair cut also, he was somewhat okay with it.

In late 1969 I was laid off from my job but right away, I got another one. This time it was a good one that I really, really liked. It was with a printing company on Front Street in Brooklyn near the Farragut Projects. It was night work, from 4:00 p.m. until 12:45 a.m., Monday through Friday. It was a twenty-minute walk from home, and I made ninety-six dollars a week. Although I liked my job, coming home at 1:00 a.m. was scary. Still, I had to work; the Housing Authority had raised our rent to fifty-two dollars a month. (That was a lot of money back then.)

For Christmas 1969, everyone went to Alabama to visit for a week, I did not go, I stayed home. On January 1, 1969, I started watching college football, and when 1970 came in, I was still watching football. It was the very first time in my life that I watched all the college bowl games—they were good games for three days.

Mary now was carrying our third little one. I had asked her if we could have another baby that I could help raise from infancy, since I was away when Claude Jr. was born and had to leave Sheryl one month after her birth. The baby was due in June 1970. I was still working at Bourum and Peace Printing Company when I got in trouble with the law for the first time since I left home in 1962. A coworker sold me a cheap gun on the job. I knew I should not have it, but being hard-headed, I started carrying it around. In April 1970, the police caught me with it, and I was locked up for one week before anyone knew where I was. At that time, it was very hard to get a call to your family if you were in jail. My brothers looked all over for me, even at the morgue. They put up posters that indicated I was missing. The only way I got through to my family was by asking a fellow prisoner who was getting out if he could call my wife and let her know where I was. He did, and on that day, Good Friday 1970, my brothers Willie and Lester came for me.

Willie had just got paid, and he used his paycheck to bail me out. I was so happy to see my family. I had made a huge mistake that I regret today. I lost my job—after all, I could not even call in for one week, and my boss thought I quit. He did not know I was in jail. I soon got another job with Drum Printing Company on Eighteenth Street in Manhattan, where I was working when little Cindy Yvette came into the world on June 28, 1970—a warm Sunday. We had come to the hospital on Saturday night and were told the baby would be here soon. However, I had to leave to stay with Sheryl and Claude Jr. On Sunday, the hospital called to let me know the baby had been born.

My brothers Willie and Lester were visiting me at the time. Lester and I walked over to Cumberland Hospital—that was on Auburn and North Portland Avenue, one block from home and the same place where Sheryl and Claude Jr. had been born. Mary told me we had a girl. We had already decided that if it was a girl, the name would be Cindy Yvette. She'd been born around 10:13 a.m. and weighed seven pounds, five ounces. What caught my eye right away was that she looked just like her mother. Out of all the babies in the nursery, she was the only one wide awake and screaming at the top of her lungs. My brother said, "Claude, this one is going to be a talker," and he was right. All her teachers told us every year that Cindy was a very bright student, but her only problem was she loved to talk. Every time I would hear this, it would take me back to what my brother said when we saw her in the hospital nursery.

As the kids continued to grow, Mary and I would bring them to the park, or all of us would go to the movies or visit family. Many days we would just stay home and play in the house. Both Mary and I continued to study with Jehovah's Witnesses. She was much more regular at it than I was. Although I knew it to be the truth, I was still trying to hold on to some worldly habits.

I wanted to have Thanksgiving dinners, put up Christmas trees, give out presents, put up lights, and sing holiday songs, but due to my Bible teaching I just did not feel right. In 1977, we stopped having a tree. I could never get my trees to stand erect, even when using a support stand. I took this as a sign from Jehovah that it was not right in his eyes for me to celebrate this day.

The autumn of 1970 began the flu season, and it was a very bad year for the flu. So many people were sick, and many died. In fact, both Mary and I were very sick at the same time, and both of us were in bed with fever. We could not take care of the kids. My sister-in-law Betty lived nearby, and she was able to come for them. Little Sheryl had to be a big girl and open the door for her. That's how sick we were.

This same year I started new work in a parking garage. This was new to me. For one, I was not a good driver at this time, and most cars in the garage were standard shift, meaning it was necessary to use a clutch—and I could not use one. In order to keep the job, which I needed very bad, I would always get my brother Willie. We worked the same shift, three days a week—and he would move the cars for me. After some time, I caught on how to drive a standard shift.

Although 1971 started out very good, in February, Mary's sister Lila died in Brooklyn; the remains were to be sent to her home in Greenville, Alabama, to be buried. My boss, however, would not give me the three days needed to travel, even though two of my coworkers were going to fill in for me. In fact, he made it clear that if I went, I would have no job to come back to. I was stuck between a rock and a hard place. Should I support my wife and family and lose my job, or should I allow her to travel alone, with small kids, to bury her sister? I chose to travel with her, knowing full well I'd just lost my job.

When we returned five days later, I started searching for work. Two days later, I received a reply from the Veterans Hospital, offering me a part-time job from 4:00 p.m. until 8:00 p.m., five days a week. I did not accept it, however, because it was a long travel from our apartment to the hospital. Also, the pay I'd have received could not support a family and pay rent. So I continued to look. I found a few dead-end jobs here and there but nothing solid. During this time, Mary was pregnant again but miscarried, which hurt us very deeply, even to this day.

In 1972 we found joy in the fact that Sheryl was now in kindergarten, and Claude Jr. was in pre-kindergarten. We did not want them to be away from home on weekday mornings, but it was good for them—and double good for Cindy, because now she could play baby all by herself.

That part ended for Cindy on August 4, 1973, when at 4:47 a.m., a crystal-clear morning, another girl was presented to us. She weighed in at seven pounds, four ounces, and we named her Crystal Dawn, because she was born in the dawn of morning, and the sky was crystal clear. She was a good baby. She sported an Afro as a baby—and a large one at that. After she was able to crawl, she loved to follow her sisters around the house. But she was a baby for only one year, because in August 1974, she was knocked out of that spot.

Honorable Discharge

from the Armed Forces of the United States of America

This is to certify that

MCQUEEN CLAUDE B ████████ SP4 USAR

was Honorably Discharged from the

United States Army

on the 1ST day of MAY 1973 This certificate is awarded as a testimonial of Honest and Faithful Service

LOUIS J. PROST
BRIGADIER GENERAL, USA

My mother was having health problems. She continued to live alone near my sister and her family in North Carolina. We all wanted Mom to come North with all her boys, but Mother was used to her quiet life in the country and would never change to city life. She would visit from time to time, and we would have so much fun with her in the house.

Mommy and Mary were more than mother-in-law/daughter-in-law; they were the best of friends. On her last visit, she pulled me aside and told me what a fine jewel I had and for me to take care of her. During 1974, Mary was carrying our daughter Caroline (although we did not know it was a girl at the time). In July 1974, I wanted to visit Mommy in North Carolina, but Mary was having complications with the pregnancy, and the doctor wanted to admit her for observation. He assured us that it was only for precautionary measures. I wanted to cancel my trip, but Mary said no, she wanted me to go visit Mommy. She said she would be just fine and that her sister Ella would bring her home after discharge and live in the house until I returned.

So on July 3, 1974, I packed one large trunk and two suitcases for the trip by Greyhound bus with Sheryl, Claude Jr., Cindy, and Crystal. We went by the hospital so Mary could see the kids from the window and wave good-bye. My brother Johnnie and one of his friends were hired to assist us—yes, I had to pay them. We made it to Port Authority, and that's where Johnnie and his friend left me right away. It was hot and there was a huge crowd, but I was able to keep control of my kids and luggage. I kept the baby, Crystal (11 months old), sitting on the trunk, with Cindy (2 years old) standing behind the trunk, with me in back of her and with Sheryl (7 years old) and Claude jr. (6 years old) on each side of me, sitting on the suitcases. And we would move forward in the line, inch by inch. After what seemed like forever, we were on the bus. I gave the older kids a snack and gave Crystal her bottle and went out to tag our luggage.

We had a great trip. We stopped in Richmond, Virginia, and I left to get soda. The cleaning crew wanted to move the bus to clean it and gas it up, but my kids let them know very clearly and loud that they were not leaving without their father. When I came back with the soda, the other passengers on the bus said, "Your kids screamed to the top of their lungs, and the cleaning crew had to leave our bus and do another."

We had fun in North Carolina. Mary called and told us she was home; we were happy about that.

Mommy was in failing health, but she was able to hold her grandkids and feed Crystal good old greasy corn bread, a favorite in the South in those days. I called all my brothers and told them Mommy's condition and asked them all to come home, which they all did. We all took Mommy to the doctor; he said she was all right. I had to leave Mommy after two weeks. She was weak on the day the kids and I left, but my sister, Daisy, was still there with her so she would not be alone. I did not want to leave the one person who had given me so very much affection, but I could tell in her eyes that she wanted me to return to Mary with the kids. I kissed Mommy good-bye and let the kids all kiss her. She said "Bye-bye" from her bed. One month later, she would be dead.

The night Mommy died, August 18, 1974, the phone rang a little after midnight. I did not answer because I thought it was my brother Lester, out drinking and wanting me to join him. But the phone kept ringing, and Mary said I should answer it because it could be an emergency. But I was very stubborn, and I was so sure it was Lester and that he was drunk that I would not answer.

Soon it stopped ringing, but two hours later, around 2:00 a.m., there was a knock at the door. Mary made me go to the door, and as I peeked out the peephole, I could see my brothers Lester and Johnnie standing there. And both of them looked very sober. I knew now that something was very wrong; this was an emergency. When I opened the door, the look in their eyes was not good. Lester said, "Why wouldn't you answer the phone? We came to let you know that Mommy just died." I felt such pain and hurt at the news, not only at losing my mother in death but by causing my brothers to travel in the dead of night from East New York and Bedford Stuyvesant—two very tough neighborhoods—to Fort Greene, another tough neighborhood, when all I had to do was answer my phone. This was all before answering machines were popular. They stayed until daylight. I was hurt by my actions for a long time. I could have gotten my brothers hurt by not answering the phone that night.

Mary was in the very last month of the pregnancy, but we made arrangements for Mother's funeral. Mary said she wanted to be there also; she wanted to support me. Our doctor advised us that she could go in labor on the road or least before we returned to New York, but we wanted to take the chance. We all traveled in one car, with my brother Curtiss doing all the driving.

After the funeral all my brothers quickly returned to New York because of their jobs. I had no job to return to at this time, so Mary, the kids, and I said we would stay the week in North Carolina and leave on Friday afternoon. I wanted to get in a last day of fishing before we got on the Greyhound bus at 7:00 p.m. for a long overnight ride to New York. Mary said she was okay and felt the trip would be no problem for her. I picked up some borrowed fishing tackle and off I went to a nearby creek where I'd fished as a boy.

But I did a stupid thing. Along the way, I stopped by a local 7-Eleven store, and of all things to buy, I bought some cheap wine and beer to take with me.

It was a very hot day. I started fishing and drinking, but I could not rest or relax, wondering if Mary was okay at home, with the heat and no air conditioning. About 1:00 p.m., I couldn't take it anymore. I started back to the house to check on everyone, walking a short distance and then taking a cab the rest of the way. As soon as I arrived home, I knew we were in trouble. Mary was sweating heavily and said she was in labor. I rushed out to the yard to ask my brother-in-law for a ride to the rescue station in town, so we could get to the hospital, which was almost ten miles away. He said his brakes were not good on the car, and he was afraid to drive. I said I would drive it, so my sister, my niece Diana, and I got Mary in the car for the ride to the emergency station. When we got there, however, the crew was out on another call. The only thing the dispatcher could do was radio for a police escort. Then I explained that my brakes were not good for a ten-mile high-speed trip and that I had wine and beer in my system. The radio car had pulled in front of me, with the red and blue light flashing, and he waved for me to follow him—he was clearing the way of traffic.

I did not know my way to the hospital so I had to stay close to him. At least I did not have to test the brakes. However, he only escorted me to the county line, which was as far as he legally could go. He had already radioed for another state trooper to pick me up and escort me to the hospital emergency section. Mary was holding her own very well. All of a sudden, I saw the hospital in the distance. I was wondering if I'd be able to stop this car. Would the state trooper see that I'd been drinking?

I could see the emergency room was on somewhat of a hill, and there was a circle driveway. My plan was to get close to the door, then pull the emergency brakes on the car and at the same time, use the curb to stop me. But Jehovah my God was with me. As I got near the door I could see nurses and men in white hospital gowns waiting for me. So at the right moment, I turned the car off, and it slowly rolled to a stop.

As quickly as it did, someone pushed a stretcher to the door of the car, and a doctor was already placing an intravenous drip in Mary's arm. Less than five minutes later, Mary was wheeled away—it was a storybook scene, I must say. After making sure she was resting okay, I was able to get the car back to my brother-in-law and check on Sheryl, Claude Jr., Cindy, and Crystal. I fed them and let them know about their mother. After getting them in bed, I returned to the hospital. Thankfully, my niece Inez and her boyfriend saw me walking along this dangerous highway and picked me up and drove me to the hospital.

When I got there, I was not permitted to see Mary right away. I was asked to have a seat in the waiting room, and I would be called. I asked the nurse if she could just tell Mary I was here, and she did. I fell asleep, and when I awoke, it was daylight outside. I'd slept all night. I asked again to see Mary and was brought in to see her. Mary told me we'd had a girl, and I was happy. We named her Caroline, after her grandmother—my mother—whose funeral we had come to attend. I later learned that the doctor who'd signed my mother's death certificate was the brother of the doctor who delivered Caroline.

After Mary and Caroline were discharged, they stayed at Mommy's house with Sheryl, Claude Jr., Cindy, and Crystal while I returned to New York to get my VA pension check. I was very broke and had just enough for a bus ticket and a subway ride to Brooklyn. When I reached the Jay Street station in Brooklyn, I had a feeling that something was wrong. As soon as I opened the door to our building in the Fort Greene projects, I found out what was worrying me. On the floor before me was all the mail scattered about, and right away I knew my check was gone.

A neighbor was standing in the lobby, and he said, "Claude, they got all of us." Everyone who was expecting a check that day lost it to a mail thief. I felt helpless. I had no money to return to North Carolina for my family. It would take two months for the government to investigate and send a replacement check. I did not have the nerve to start asking for help from anyone because no one had money. Times were tough on everyone. But it seemed like I was the worst off. My family was stuck in North Carolina, and someone had just stolen my only means to support them. What would I do?

I always was a very prideful and independent person. But now I had to swallow my pride and depend on help from others. I started by asking the only people I could: my brothers Willie and Lester. Between two of them they found enough for me to return to get my family. Even then, I still had to pawn my wife's wedding rings and my watch to make enough for all the bus tickets needed. It was a blessing that six of us left New York and now seven of us were returning two weeks later. Caroline was the only one who was not born in the Cumberland Hospital. She was born in Moore County Memorial Hospital, Pinehurst, North Carolina—the golf capital of the world.

My dad was such a great help for us during this hardship. He gave his best in the way of food items. He never held a regular job, but when he was not in jail for running bootleg whiskey, he held odd jobs, cleaning yards or painting houses, whatever he could get. Dad and I never had a father/ son relationship when I was growing up. However, late in 1974 I asked him to come visit, which he accepted, and at this time I was able to hear his reasons for why he had not been around for me. It hurt me, not seeing him year after year, and most of all when I would overhear someone speak badly about him, such as calling him a drunk or a bootlegger—I knew these words were bad. But when Dad sat with me and talked to me, then I had a better understanding.

So, I say to all fathers, you must spend quality time with your sons and daughters from birth until death. It is very important for a father to be present in the very best way he can, not only with gifts but in the way of instruction.

By 1975 we had a growing family and needed more space. We had two bedrooms but we needed three and in February 1975, we were able to move into a three-bedroom apartment at 124 Carlton Avenue. That same month, Mary was baptized as one of Jehovah's Witnesses. I did not attend her baptism; I stayed home with the children. That day gave us all hope because we started learning about the Creator more intensively. We both continued to study the Bible. Mary made more progress than I did. I would attend some meetings but not regularly. When I did attend meetings, I truly loved being there. It was always so peaceful, with good conversations, and I learned things about God that I had never heard before. I just loved it. But it would be fifteen years in the future, however, before I myself would be baptized.

Each year between June and October, Jehovah's Witnesses hold conventions throughout the world to help educate those who want to know about God, whose name we know to be Jehovah. At this time, the conventions were held on Friday, Saturday, and Sunday from around 9:30 a.m. until around 5:00 p.m., with a two-hour intermission for lunch and social time. The event was often held at Yankee Stadium, Belmont Racetrack, or assembly halls.

For the first few years, I did not attend, but I would watch Mary making lunch for each day for herself and other friends who had children, who would be traveling with her. I could not understand how the kids could be gone all day and still come home ready to play. In fact, I was upset that they were made to sit for that long. But Mary explained to me that I was mistaken—she said they could go to the bathroom at any time or take a break for water or to stretch their legs. She invited me to come and see for myself, which I did for the 1976 convention. I must say I enjoyed every minute of it, being in a crowd of people that size, and there was no cursing; no one was drinking or drunk. Everyone was dressed lovely; everyone was smiling, saying hello, and they were sincere. This was new to me. I wanted to return to being with people of all races, young and old, boys and girls, men and women—it just made a difference in my life.

This was unlike when I had attended churches where the people made fun of someone if his clothes were not up to fashion or if he drove an old car. In the other churches, some people could not converse with certain groups who thought little of them because of their schooling or because they did not have curly hair. That was the way it was in the church. I never felt welcome, but here, people talked to me as if they had known me for years, even though we had just met. This was the way I'd always dreamed life to be.

I would get odd jobs here and there, and somehow we made it. Sheryl was now nine years old, Claude Jr. was eight, Cindy was six, Crystal was three, and Caroline was two. Claude Jr. was complaining more and more that he had no one to play with because he didn't have a brother. I did what I could to fill in the gap by playing with him, but it wasn't the same; he wanted a brother. So before long, we were expecting again, and we were looking for a boy.

We spent the summer of 1976 enjoying each day in Fort Greene Park with balls, bikes, and jump ropes. We would always go together when we had hot nights—too hot to be in the house without fans or air conditioning. Mary and I would sit on benches outside our building and let the kids play until nine or ten o'clock at night. Even when the weather cooled down somewhat, we never left the kids unattended or with neighbors to watch. That was our job, and we did it.

September was always a big month for us, as it was for any parent who had school-aged kids. The merchants loved this month—school clothes, notebooks, pens, you name it. Thanks to Jehovah, we were always able to function quite well. We would plan in advance and save a little money each month before the first day of school day. It was not always easy, and there were a few times when we didn't have everything the children needed to start school—pens, pencils, notebooks, clothes, etc.—but each year became a learning year. Most important, we always made parent/teacher night. Everyone knew me as the only father to show up at each meeting in a suit and tie. I wanted to show respect, not only for my kids but for the entire school. All parents should make room to meet with their kids' teachers. This is so very important.

Sheryl, Claude Jr., and Cindy were attending P.S. 46 in Brooklyn, on Clermont Avenue, directly across the street from our Kingdom Hall, where we had our Bible worship. We were awaiting the arrival of our new one, wondering if it would be a boy or a girl. December 1976 was a blustery, light-snow month. That's just the way it was on the day Mary went into labor on December 28. On that day, Claude Jr. got his brother—and he was so very happy about it. We named him Clark Marcus. He was a very nosy little guy. When his mother would feed him in the hospital room, he would always have one eye open, checking out everything, but he was also a sweet baby. He didn't cry too often, but when he did, look out—he never let up until he got his bottle. Clark was the one who stayed close to his mother. She could not do anything without holding him. She cooked with him in her arms. She washed dishes with him under her feet. If she would go to shower, he would scream his head off until she opened the bathroom door and let him in. When she would sit to eat, she had to hold him. He just wanted to be near his mother at all times. But he also was a good baby—very creative, he could make his own play things, which he often liked more than store-bought toys.

Clark was very active from day one. As he grew older, we always said Clark could do everything—football, basketball, volleyball, gymnastics, high-jump, low-jump, somersaults. This kid was the daring one; he would take chances you would not believe. Sometimes he would catch me off guard and scare me to death with his actions, such as jumping off the top bunk bed at the age of two. He made it look simple, but for Mom and Dad, he made early gray hair appear.

The years 1977 and 1978 were great in some ways but not so great in others. I didn't have a full-time job, but it was great to be home with the family every day; great to walk my kids to school and pick them up from school; great to have quality time in the park together. But money was tight, and there were no jobs to be had. Beyond our own family financial situation, it was during these years that a subway and bus strike shut down the city, and a gas shortage affected those who drove cars. And then there was a citywide blackout that put the New York City in ruins due to the widespread looting and arson.

Our seventh child was due in April. My birthday is April 10, Sheryl's is April 14, and my brother Lester's is April 27. Would the baby be born on one of our birthdays? We were looking forward to it. But that did not happen. On a lovely night, April 29, we were presented with another boy, all of seven pounds, three ounces of him. We had thought to give the baby a "C" name, like the rest of the family. But one of our neighbors suggested that we name the baby Robert—it was her late husband's name, she said, and it would make her feel so good that a baby was named after him. Mary and I talked about it and decided that yes, we would name him Robert because our neighbor had been so good to us. We still have him a "C" name, though—we named him Robert Clayton. And from the time he was an infant, everyone called him Clay.

I was looking for work every day. Some days, I would get a day or two with a temporary job here and there. Whatever I could get, I accepted. If the job was within walking distance, I would walk in order to save money to put food on the table. I always wanted my kids to have plenty to eat, to never go hungry. Also, I was still fighting a drinking problem. There were times when I could go weeks without the urge to drink, but then it would hit me, and I just did not have the strength to resist—and that would be my downfall. I would allow myself to become who I was not.

I recall one Sunday, I was drinking and ran out of money. I could not find the bank book, even though banks were not open on Sundays and of course, there were no ATMs at that time. What I wanted to do was borrow money from someone I knew, and I wanted to show I had money to repay. Mary knew where the bank book was, but she was at the Kingdom Hall of Jehovah's Witnesses. I did not want to wait until she returned home; I decided to go there to ask her where the bank book was. The streets were very tough in those years, so I reached in our kitchen drawer to take a knife with me to protect myself in the street, since I was drinking and was wobbly.

Bringing a knife had bad results. When I appeared at the hall and asked to speak to my wife, it seemed as if I was after her to fight. That was not the case, but it was something that was highly misunderstood. I have always been very sorry that it happened in the first place, but in order to not make it seem as if I were making a lame excuse for the incident, I never attempted to address it. I just let it go as people saw it.

I am extremely sorry that this happened the way it did. I considered this to be a lesson learned. It showed what could happen when things were not well thought out beforehand and the embarrassment that it can cause for many years to come.

The year 1980 started out extremely well for us. Most of our children were in school all day, except for the two who were not yet old enough for school. Mary had her hands full. Every morning she would walk the older ones to school, with the younger ones in tow. Then she'd return home to make beds, clean house, and prepare dinner, because she wanted a hot meal every day for the kids when they came home from school. She would always help them with their homework. When Robert (Clay) started to crawl, he loved to follow his two brothers around the house. We boys would wrestle on the floor, having great fun together but always were careful not to be too rough or hurt little Clay Clay.

Clark was always the tough one. Clay would do everything Clark did, up to a point. I would always try to bring home Matchbox cars and trucks, as well as other toys throughout the year to help entertain everyone. On cold, rainy, or snowy days, I would make a playhouse for the girls out of bed sheets and give them some of their mother's pots and pans to play with.

At this time we only had a thirteen-inch black-and-white TV to share among us, but this was good because it kept us close. I would search the TV guide in the paper for family shows that we could enjoy together. The girls liked to watch *The Brady Bunch* after school. The boys liked mostly cartoons. Mary would always have Kool-Aid for us to enjoy. When the snow would come, we would dress the baby in a snowsuit and go outside. We'd take the very top of the snow, put it in a bowl, and add cinnamon and sugar, vanilla flavoring, and Carnation milk, and make ice cream the old-fashioned way. Then we'd enjoy it together.

All the children had friends who would come to visit. Sheryl had Johanna; Claude Jr. had Reginald; Cindy had Vernetta; Crystal had

John; Caroline had Taiya; Clark had Raymond; and Clay had everyone. Everyone was happy. I was now working at the job I would hold for the next thirty years.

I'd had no choice but to leave the printing trade where I'd been working, because the noise from the presses gave me the impression that guns were being fired and even though I used earplugs, I was a nervous wreck; my nerves were not good.

I think only other combat vets (or those people who work in the VA hospitals with combat vets) can truly appreciate and fully understand the deep emotional trauma that resulted from our time in Vietnam. Other people in our daily lives don't see the hurt, because for the "lucky" ones who returned from Vietnam with their physical bodies intact, there are no apparent reminders. But I think all veterans of the Vietnam conflict came home with major problems. Some soldiers did lose limbs or were otherwise badly wounded, but others—and I am included in this group—suffered emotional wounds that could not be seen, whether it was nervousness caused by loud noises or having a guilty conscience over ever being involved in such a war. I know I hadn't wanted to be physically hurt, and I surely did not want to hurt anyone else. But that was war, and although I came home in "one piece," the Vietnam conflict left its scars on me.

I had to take care of a family, so I took whatever work came along. I had no training in jobs such as being a bookkeeper, auto mechanic, or taxi driver; I could not get such jobs. I also spent a lot of time going to a doctor at the VA hospital, which limited my ability to work, but when I was well enough mentally to get work, I had to take whatever I could get to support my family.

The early 1980s ('81–'85) introduced the world to two new killers that mankind had not known before: crack cocaine and HIV. The doctors in the hospitals were baffled by this new virus confronting them, even as young thugs fought over "turf," battling each other for the right to sell drugs in a certain area. The result was often many gunfights in my neighborhood, and crack cocaine seemed to be everywhere you looked.

Before this era, very few young men or women went to jail for drug-related problems. Also before this era, HIV was unheard of, but suddenly people in the gay community started dying. The doctors did not have an answer. The police did not have an answer.

However, as a husband and father, I knew I had to act quickly and build a tough defense around my family to protect them. Mary and I talked about ways we could work together with our kids to protect them. We decided that the number one way was to keep them coming to the meetings at the Kingdom Hall. This way, they would hear instructions on how to live a good, clean life. This would be delivered to them from God's word, the Bible. We lived in a tough neighborhood, Fort Greene, Brooklyn. Back in the '80s, the rich did not invest in our neighborhood. No one with money wanted to risk losing it on a neighborhood like Fort Greene. There were too many project people; too many welfare people. Even the police were nervous about being there sometimes.

But look at the same neighborhood today, 2011, there are high-rise buildings, a new culture of people, fine restaurants, new stores, and new parking regulations. This is the same neighborhood that no one wanted in 1980. What happened? The rich with money decided to go together and buy the entire neighborhood.

~A NEW WAY OF LIFE~

The early part of 1985 was very cold—one of the coldest in memory. I was working six days a week, sixty-plus hours. My only day off was Sunday. We spent our cold days after school and work watching TV. We all watched a doo-wop show or *Sanford and Son*. My job was very busy at this time. I was running the only public parking garage in the south Brooklyn Heights neighborhood. We did a heavy load every day. So when I would reach home, I would be exhausted. However, I would make myself stay awake for some quality time with the family.

At this time I still was dealing with a heavy drinking problem, and drinking dulls the mind. So along with the drinking, I would gamble with lotto or play day numbers or horse races. This was a form of being greedy. I did not have to do this, because I had a full-time job. It was a way to entertain myself, to see if I could make a hit for more money. The end result was that I found out a person who drinks never heals until he quits. A gambler is always a loser, even if he wins. I knew I had to work on these problems. I wanted dearly to become a Jehovah's Witness and knew from my study of the Bible that these things were not allowed in the congregation.

But first I had another problem: I was trying to stop smoking at this time. I had been smoking for twenty-eight years. I started on the farm, smoking rabbit tobacco rolled up in brown paper. Rabbit tobacco is a wild weed that looks somewhat like tobacco. Young boys on the farm would use this because Mom and Dad did not allow boys to smoke until they were at least sixteen years old.

I had tried many times to stop smoking, but it never lasted more than a day before I was right back to it. I was now having problems breathing or walking up hills without becoming tired. I knew it was because of smoking. But how could I quit? After all, I was buying two packs a day. I would break the filter off so I could get all the hard taste. I smoked Marlboro at this time. Over all, I used ten different brands during my years of smoking. But now I had to find a way to stop. My brother Willie had died at age fifty-four from lung cancer in November 1983. This gave me every reason to stop—or it should have.

I told people that I quit smoking cold turkey. That's true, but where did I get the strength? Jehovah God gave it to me. I could never have done it on my own, because I had already tried many times, and it didn't work. So surely a higher power was behind my success. This is how it happened. I came home on Sunday, February 13, 1984, after an all-night drinking tour with so-called friends. It was midday, and my wife and all the kids were just on their way to the congregation meeting. Everyone looked so nice in their suits, and everyone greeted me. The girls all gave me a big hug and kiss on the cheek. So did my wife. She also said that dinner was ready on the stove, if I wanted to eat.

I felt awful watching them leave for the meeting without me. Not only should I have been with them, but I also should have been the leader. I was in a low state and didn't feel good about not being with them. Now I was out of money, out of liquor, out of smokes. By the time the family returned home, I had cleaned myself up, but I could not bring myself to ask my wife for cigarette money. I said to myself, *If I can only make it through this night without smoking, I will get money at my job tomorrow.* Well, it was hard. I even remember going out in the hallway, looking for loose butts so I could remove the tobacco and roll a cigarette in paper.

The morning came—I'd made it through the night without smoking. Now I could go to work and get money from the boss. But that did not work out either. My boss was broke; his wife had shopped over the weekend. That day we did not get even one cash-paying customer for the whole day, which was very unusual in this type of business. The result of the day was that February 13, 1984, was the last day I had a cigarette in my mouth. Thanks to Jehovah God. He gets credit for helping me quit smoking by the way things went. I may have stopped cold turkey, but he is the one who helped me keep it that way.

In July 1984 we had the one and only family reunion in my life. It was held in Southern Pines, North Carolina. It was great. We used a charter bus from New York for all the family here who were able to go. When we arrived in North Carolina, we met up with family from all over the United States. We met family I never knew about.

Good food, good social events—I truly enjoyed everything. The one thing I most remember was after we returned to New York, Mary said that when she noticed I had a drink and did not smoke, she knew at that time I had fully given up smoking. Shortly afterward my lungs began to heal. I found myself with new energy. I could walk up hills and climb stairs without huffing and puffing so much. But the desire for a cigarette had a strong pull. Sometimes the nicotine pull was so strong, I felt like if only I could get one pull on a cigarette, I would be all right. Sometimes I would become nauseated because I had smoked for twenty-eight years and stopped cold turkey. My body was crying out for what it was used to.

But I was not going to give in. I had come too far to turn back now. It now has been twenty-seven years since I last smoked. I feel great, even today. If I am around someone smoking now, I can't take it. The year 1985 came in like a lion, with a very cold and snowy winter. We had two or three snowstorms each month in January, February, and March of that year. I was working long hours in garage management, and some days the load was heavy. But I wanted my family to have good things, so I would work every day from 4:30 a.m. to 5:00 p.m. I never failed to open for twelve years straight.

All the kids were doing so well in school—Sheryl in music; Claude Jr. and Cindy in art; Crystal and Caroline making honor roll; Clark and Robert getting good grades on tests. All this gave me good reason to be a hard worker on my job. Mary had her full-time job also. She would have a hot meal ready every day when the kids came in from school. She would always have a listening ear for all the things they talked about and encourage them to do their homework. Then she would check the work and have them correct the wrong points. Then she would wash dishes and clean the house, sometimes as late as midnight, before going to bed.

There are verses in God's word, the Bible, that describe the type of wife, mother, and homemaker she was:

> *A capable wife who can find her? Her value is far more than that of corals.*
>
> —Proverbs 31:10

> *She has rewarded him with good and not bad all the days of her life. … She has proved to be like the ships like the merchant, from far away she brings in her food.*
>
> —Proverbs 31:12, 14

> *Her mouth she has opened in wisdom. And the law of loving kindness is upon her tongue.*
>
> —Proverbs 31:26

In summer 1985 we enjoyed a family vacation to Greenville, Alabama, Mary's hometown. We always spent at least one week on vacation, getting out of the city life. Some of the kids did not like the heat, bugs, and slow pace of the country. They still feel the same way as adults.

That same summer, 1985, at one of our conventions, a book called *Reasoning* from the Scriptures was released to all who attended. Right away I found this book to be very useful. I found so many things about which I had once had the wrong view. Now I could clearly see the truth of the matter, such as God's view on marriage, sex, holidays, and blood. These can be hard subjects to understand on one's own, but after looking at it from the Creator's view, things changed for a clearer point of view.

I still use this book today to help me guide my life. The year 1986 started out with many young men in our neighborhood losing their lives to the streets. It seemed that although they were smart young men with good grades in school, they suddenly turned to what they saw as an easy, get-rich-quick life on the streets. They gave up their chance for a good, clean life and chose a life with no future. It hurt me to see things like this going on, because they were young and had so much to live for. Some were schoolmates of my kids, but one important thing was missing in most of the cases. What was that? It's sad to say, but it was that the father was missing from the home. The mother can only do so much alone. The father plays a very important part in a child's life, whether girl or boy. If the father is missing, then the leader that God has put as head of the house cannot be followed.

I have said the same thing to all my sons, my grandsons, my great-grandsons, and all males who become fathers: stick with your kids. Teach them, guide them, and spend time with them. In this way you will become more than a father to them. You will be their king and prince and a highly respected one in their lives. They need you to be there for them.

In the summer of 1986, the city of New York gave permission for the only Vietnam veterans' parade in New York. All veterans were invited to attend a march across the Brooklyn Bridge to Battery Park to the Vietnam Memorial. I wanted to be with the crowd, and although Mary did not, she still came with me. There were hundreds of veterans in uniform, some in the jungle-type uniform we used in the war. As we crossed the bridge, many people were standing along the railing, cheering us on. I was dressed in combat boots, army jacket, and beret and had all my medals pinned to my chest. About midway across the bridge, I started taking off my medals and giving them away. People were amazed that I would do this.

But I wanted no more to do with the unjust war. I know for a fact that my actions were because of my Bible training. Thus, my medals, combat rope, and hat were given away on the Brooklyn Bridge march. I even wanted to step out of my combat boots and walk away from them, but I had no other shoes to put on. The only thing I had left after that day was my uniform and boots.

I was still dealing with the problem of drinking, and sometimes it would get far out of control. There were mornings when as soon as my eyes opened, I would reach for the bottle of hard liquor without breakfast or juice. I would turn the bottle up to my mouth, drink a big swallow, wash up, dress, and head to work. Mary did such a great job in helping me to see this was not good but most times, I would give her a hard time, and she would leave me alone. But I know today that she was praying for me to find a way to stop. God answered her prayers, because I stopped drinking for good after being arrested for driving while intoxicated in 1988. I spent a night and a day in the nasty, filthy, urine-smelling lock-up with a cell full of hardened criminals. If I got thirsty, the only water was in the commode. I did not get thirsty.

When I got out, that's when the shameful, humiliating effect of it hit me. I had to give up my driver's license, pay a heavy fine, and go to school three nights a week for two hours, for six months. Plus, my car insurance went up extremely high for three years. This really put me to shame. I could only drive to and from work. What a waste of money, time, and reputation. That did it for me.

I did continue to drink for a while afterward but not any more behind the wheel of a car. But shortly thereafter, I found out I had high blood pressure, and I was placed on medication. I knew I could not mix liquor and this medication. Also, I looked closer at how God looked at a person who drinks heavily, even behind closed doors, and I found out this is not good in his eyes. I could be "disfellowshipped" from the Christian congregation for this behavior. Therefore. I knew I must stop—and stop for good.

With the smoking and drinking done away with, the gambling was not as hard to give up, because my drinking fed the desire to gamble. Today, I feel great with these things out of my life, although it's a fight to do what's right. Sometimes the desire for a drink comes to mind, but I pray for strength to overcome it. I need the help that God gives, and he is always ready to give.

The years 1987 and 1988 continued to be filled with trouble from so much drug trade, and everyone was nervous about going out of their houses, for fear of getting caught in a cross fire of bullets. We kept ourselves busy at Kingdom Hall meetings or in Fort Greene Park. Summer days were spent at my workplace, washing cars or riding bikes. The boys and I even made a few go-carts for fun. We made a nice one from an old wheelchair, and it caught attention from people in the street. We rigged it up nicely, and everyone enjoyed a ride on it.

My dad died in 1987, and I must say I was happy that he had told me the things he did before he died, so that I wasn't left wondering, not knowing why he had not been around when I was growing up. I make no excuse for him, but he never had a chance. He was a slave for most of his life. He never went to school, never learned to read or write. He had a deep love for all my kids, but Clark was his pride and joy. He said Clark reminded him of himself, being so tough and daring. When I really needed his help—such as when Caroline was born, and I was burying my mother at the same time—he had good credit at the general store, and he came to bring food for Mary and the older kids while I returned to New York. Remember, when I got to New York I found the check had been stolen. I was totally broke, but Dad gave what he could.

January 1989 was a freezing-cold month—one of the worst. There were lots of snow days to deal with. The family was growing up. Three had graduated high school already. My friend and coworker Seymour had retired and moved to Florida. I was left on my own to run the garage the best I could, but Seymour had taught me well. He'd also told me to prepare for a second company to take over, but that I could stay or leave when that time came.

I was not focused on any of that. Mary and I were looking forward to the arrival of our very first grandchild. Our daughter Cindy was expecting, and her due date was fast approaching. Everyone was happy and saying that we needed a baby in the house.

The year 1990 came in very good for me. I was beginning to feel real good about myself and that things would only be better for me. However, I found out early in 1990 that my dear friend Wallace, who was in the training school with me back in 1962, had contracted that deadly AIDS virus. He was now quite sick, and when I went to visit him, he did not look anything like the man I knew. I felt so very sorry for him. He was the closest friend I'd ever had. He was always ready to do anything for me, but now, I could not do anything for him.

When I told him of my upcoming plan to become a Jehovah's Witness, he was so happy for me. He sat up in bed and said, "Claude, you will make a good Witness, so don't turn around." Wallace would die in early

1991. I found out too late to prevent his being buried in Potters Field in a pine box and with a number. Over the years I wanted to investigate to see if his family recovered his remains and gave him a proper burial, but I never did.

As for me, the closer I got to my baptism date in February 1990, the more joy I felt. I could see the joy in Mary, too, and could tell how happy others were for me. I truly wanted to become a Jehovah's Witness. I wanted to know about God our Creator. I knew much about the way the world does things, but now I wanted to know how God does things.

On my baptismal day, I looked around me and there was my wife, my children, my brothers Curtiss, Lester, and Johnnie, and my sister, Daisy. Neither my brothers nor my sister were Jehovah's Witnesses, but they were there for me and happy for me. As I looked throughout the assembly hall, there were hundreds of others looking on—a total count of 2,203, all seeking the same thing: a close relationship with the Creator of the entire universe. What a beautiful day, indeed.

Now I was able to go door-to-door in my neighborhood, not looking to find someone to drink or gamble with, but someone to whom I could preach the word of God—and this made me feel good. I was able to sit at the dinner table and have a Bible study with my three sons, instead of trying to hide my liquor breath from them. All my four daughters could be proud to speak of their father to their friends—not that they did not do so before, but now it was more pure.

In December 1993, I almost missed out on a grand chance to do something with my wife—to take a cruise around the Caribbean Islands. At first I did not want to go because of my bad experience on the airplane from Vietnam in 1968. I just did not want to fly anymore. In order to take this cruise, I would need to fly to the island of San Juan, Puerto Rico, to board the ship.

I wanted no part of flying but after giving it close thought, I said, "Let's do it." I am happy today that I did, because as things turned out, that would be the one and only cruise that Mary and I took together. Mary passed away on June 25, 1998. To my surprise, Caroline died on August 16, 2006. However, the three of us had an enormous amount of fun on the cruise for seven days, sailing around some very beautiful islands, with good weather. I am blessed to be left with such a wonderful memory of this.

The day we returned to JFK Airport, there was snow and ice on the ground. I almost did not make the trip for another reason. That reason was because earlier that year, in June 1993, there was a break-in at my workplace. Had I not listened to Mary, I might have been coming in to work about the same time that the crime was taking place, and I surely would have been harmed or possibly killed.

The Bible teaches mankind many things to benefit him, one of which is how marriage mates should pay close attention to each other. The man should not always have the last say-so on matters, nor should the woman. God told Abraham to listen to his wife, Sarah, and Abraham did listen. And all went well for him and Sarah.

At one time, I was a man who really did not listen to my wife. I thought I had all the answers. I thought I could solve everything. But after learning so much from the Bible on this subject, I began to change my view. And never did I regret doing so, because I believe it might have helped save my life.

My customary routine every day was to leave my home between 4:00 and 4:15 a.m. on my bike, to reach my garage early enough to have coffee, read the paper, or relax a little before I would open the gates at 6:00 a.m. to start the day. This trip would put me at the garage no later than 4:45 a.m. I did not need to be in this early, but my body would automatically wake me at the same time every day, even on non-work days.

As I dressed for work, Mary asked why I was leaving so early. She said I didn't need to leave so early. "Drink your coffee at home this morning," she said. There was a time when I would have just ignored her and stubbornly continued to dress to leave. But on that day, I listened to her, sat down, and had coffee at home, which prevented my being at the garage during the break-in. A group of construction workers, angry with the way the owner had paid them for their work, had broken in, wrecked some cars and stolen others.

Afterward, by the time I arrived at the garage, the customer complaint list was heavy on my shoulders. Customers wanted to know where their cars were and who would pay for the damages. They needed their cars and wanted to know how the break-in could have happened. Believe it or not, all my supervisors and bosses ran for cover and left me with everything. I could not believe it. Eight brand-new cars had been badly damaged or totaled inside the garage. Seven brand-new cars had been removed from the garage and left in the street. And I was left all by myself to fight off these angry customers who wanted answers that I did not have. I had to deal with the police reports and insurance reports. That day I had to prove myself as a manager. I didn't get home until about 3:00 a.m. the next day.

The break-in was a police matter, but the only way I was able to withstand this pressure without strong verbal feedback was because of my Bible-based training. Without it, there would have been problems coming from me for anyone who came charging at me for something I had no control over.

I continued to enjoy going to my Christian meetings and going out in the field on Saturdays to tell all who would listen about Jehovah God and his son. Jesus Christ. It was so nice that everyone in the family would prepare to go out together on Saturday and enjoy a day in the Bible-teaching work. Afterward, we would have lunch together.

I always remembered an old saying that went like this: the family that prays together, stays together. And that's just what I always taught in our home to keep the family together.

About this time, late 1995, Mary started having health problems. She and I talked about it and made appointments to see different doctors. We did not want to upset or worry the kids, so we did not talk too much about our health around them. The two of us knew it was serious. She would tell me things that she wanted me to know. She always was a strong person, so she would not worry or let the problem get her down.

For seven years she and I worked next door to each other. She was a child-care person for two lovely kids that she raised from infancy. They grew to know her as their second mother. Norman and Rachael always were dear to our family and still are today. Mary and I would leave work around the same time and travel home together. She retired from child care in August 1997, and I gave her a retirement dinner with some of her friends.

November 14, 1997, would be our last anniversary together, although neither of us knew it would be. At this time, her mother also was ill in Alabama, and Mary would be there with her on our thirtieth wedding anniversary—we would be separated on this day. But then I said to myself, *Oh, no, not if I can help it, we won't.*

So I set a plan in motion where I would arrive in Alabama on our anniversary, and it would be a surprise. First, I sent two cards postmarked to arrive on that day. Second, I sent flowers to arrive on that day. Then I called someone in her family to help me by picking me up at the Greyhound bus station.

I told all my kids here what I had planned and that they should keep it secret. I called Mary and told her I would be working another garage for a day or two, and she could not call me but I would call her. I told her I did not know the phone number where I would be. She went along with it because she knew this was my job description from time to time.

I brought a ticket on Greyhound that arrived in Alabama at 5:00 p.m. on our anniversary. I rode the bus from 2:00 p.m. Thursday until 5:00 p.m. Friday, when I arrived in this little town of Greenville—a very small place, where everybody knows everybody. When a stranger shows up, it gets attention.

That's what happened with me. As I stepped off the bus to call my contact, none other than Mary's sister Bobbie Jean was looking at me. She lived in Greenville but did not know I was coming. I rushed up to her, assured her that yes, it was me, Claude, her brother-in-law, and said, "Don't tell Mary I am here. It's a surprise for her."

I had called Mary a few days earlier and told her a package would come by Greyhound bus, so she should be on the lookout for it. I did not tell her that I would be the package. My contact picked me up right on time, and I hid in the back of his truck. Now I called the house and asked what they were having for dinner. When Mary told me, I said, "Maybe I'll come down for some of that." She said, "How can you do that? You are in New York." I said, "I will take a super jet." She said, "Good, come on down. I'll leave some on the stove for you." She didn't know that I was only five minutes away.

My helper drove up to her mother's house and rang the doorbell. From my hiding place in the truck, I heard him tell Mary, "I picked up the package from the bus depot that you said Claude was sending, but I need help bringing it in the house. Can you help me?" I heard Mary say, "Sure, let me get my shoes." I had my camera ready, and I could hear her footsteps coming to the rear of the truck. I got a good clear photo—she was so, so startled! She did not know how I was able to pull that off on her.

We were together on our thirtieth anniversary; it would be our last together. Mary and Caroline drove me to the Greyhound bus depot that Sunday morning, and I left for New York.

I would arrive back in New York City on Monday at noon, just in time to get the car and pick up Mary and Caroline at the airport. The trip was very much a pleasure, and I was glad I used my instinct and took the trip.

Early in 1998, the doctor continued to watch Mary's health, and she and I talked constantly about it. Her mother visited us in March 1998, and it was encouraging to all of us. But we lost her suddenly on June 25, 1998. It was and still is hard to deal with. We had known each other for thirty-four years. We both knew of God's promise of a resurrection, and Mary always taught that to others. Her sister Ella died only two months later. Therefore, 1998 was a sad year for the family, but we were able to pull through because of the loving support and prayers of others.

My wife Mary gave me thirty-one years of splendor before her sudden death on June 25, 1998. Oh, how faithfully she worked with me. How respectful she was to me as her husband. She never put me down, in private or public. She always gave me praise when around her family or her close friends. Never did I come home from work and find her sloppily dressed or with her hair in rollers. Many days I knew she was not feeling too great when I would leave for work. But she always kept herself very clean. Even when she was pregnant, she was a get-up-and-go person.

She had no one to talk to for up building strength. Her family did not share her Christian beliefs. In fact, most of them belittled her for choosing the Jehovah's Witness faith. They really talked down to her.

But she held her ground and by doing so, she left behind after her death a strong family. She also helped all seven children to come to love Jehovah, to live the Christian way of life. Without her in my life, I don't think I could have made it so far in my life. She gave me the boost when I needed to be jump-started.

I can never forget the years of drinking and days of depression and how she comforted me; how she would clean my vomit from the floor after I would be sick from overdrinking. She never tried to embarrass me or call me bad names. She loved Jehovah and the things she was learning about him.

When she was not busy cooking or cleaning and the kids were relaxed, she would be studying. Once or twice I said to her, "You are studying too hard. Take a break." She would always say back to me, "No, Claude, it's when I'm not studying that it's hard."

Oh, what a person she was. Even people who would meet me for the first time, witnesses or non-witnesses, would always say good things about her. How I was blessed to have such a person in my life. Mary proved this in the way she carried herself, that she was conscious of her spiritual need. No matter what confronted her in daily life, she allowed God's way to lead her.

Her faith was so strong that shortly before her death, she asked me to not worry about her. She knew she was sick. We talked at night when the kids were sleep. She was more concerned for me. She asked me to not divert from the direction to do God's will.

She was so happy when she received the invitation to attend the 1998 August pioneer school. But sadly, she fell asleep in death before it was accomplished. The family was encouraged by her spirit as well as the example that she set. Mary always thanked me for supporting her. She mentioned that this was by far one of the happiest times of her life. I certainly am looking forward to seeing her again in the new life that awaits those who fall asleep in death, doing the work of God faithfully.

I recall many times when I said, "I must do this not my way but the way the Bible says do it." But one time stands out to me. I had just walked out of a Key Food Supermarket in downtown Brooklyn, and there, in full view on a snow bank, was a brown leather man's wallet. I stopped for a moment and looked at it, not knowing if this was a police setup, and they were waiting to arrest anyone who picked it up, or if someone actually had lost the wallet. I picked it up, put it in my pocket, and walked the short distance to my job, where I looked inside the wallet for a number to call.

Inside the wallet was photo identification, driver's license, seven major credit cards, gas cards, birth certificate, and a piece of paper with PINs corresponding to credit cards. There were seven one-hundred-dollar bills, four fifty-dollar bills, three twenty-dollar bills, three ten-dollar bills, and three five-dollar bills. Also, there were photos of a smiling family of five. Before I learned the way of the Bible, I am sure I would have just removed the cash and dropped the wallet in a mailbox.

But here's what I did. I looked at the driver's license, and the address on it was not so far from my workplace. So I started calling telephone numbers that were in the wallet. I asked to speak to the person whose name was on the driver's license. It was he who answered the phone.

I asked if he'd lost his wallet, but he insisted that he hadn't lost it. In fact, he told me to stop calling him. I assured him that I was holding his wallet, that I had found this wallet in the snow on Atlantic Avenue about an hour ago and that I wanted to return it to its owner. He asked me to wait a minute. He left the phone, but very soon I heard the sound of running feet. He picked up the phone and said in a frantic voice. "Where are you? That's my wallet. I need it!"

I told him that all he needed to do was tell me some of the things in the wallet so I would know it was his; then I'd bring it to him. He named every credit card and gave me the same address that was on the license. I brought his wallet to him and asked that he check the wallet for everything and count the money. He did; then he said he wanted me to take a reward, but I refused. He tried to press me to accept a reward, to take what was not mine. I still refused, and when I pulled away, he was still standing in the street, scratching his head in disbelief. I must admit that money looked good. No one knew I'd found it and to keep it would seem like the natural thing to do. But I couldn't have kept it and had a good conscience.

Many people have asked me why I did not just throw the wallet in the snow or into a mailbox and keep the money. Well, the answer is simple: it was not mine. My obligation was to try to find the rightful owner, which I did. This is doing things God's way and not the way man may do things.

My job as manager of a parking garage began in 1980, and I have managed the same garage under two different owners for over thirty years. In this line of work, the opportunity to steal, cheat, lie, or mislead is always present. I am happy with myself that I have worked hard to maintain a clean record in this regard.

Over the years I have been confronted by those who wanted to bribe me with cash to give up a select parking space, and when I let them know I do not accept bribes, they've looked at me as if to say I must be crazy not to accept the money. Even my employers have used spy operations or decoy workers to see who can be caught stealing from the company. Sad to say, but some have been caught doing just that.

I let it be known early in my career that I would not be pulled into covering up or lying for any fellow worker, customer, or employer. If a car was damaged in my garage, I did not try to hide it from a customer. I always said, "That's why the garage has insurance." But for the most part, I always tried to have a damage-free garage.

To add to that, each of my employers over the years has voiced approval of the way the business is run. This means so very much to me.

But I do not take credit for having a good record of managing on my own record. The credit goes to a higher power, who taught me to be the way I am. The transformation that Jehovah God has helped me to undergo has truly made me humble, kind, approachable, understanding, and able to speak the truth from the heart.

I try to always be an example to my coworkers—not so much as a boss but a coworker. I'm ready to come away from the desk and share in the necessary work, whether it was sweeping the floor, taking out garbage, or cleaning the restroom. I tried to be part of it all. Throughout the years in this work, I have worked with well over 250 different workers, where my staff calls for only seven workers. But I am happy to say I helped many to become managers of their own garages, and some are still within the company. They will reach out to me from time to time, to thank me for the help they received.

Others have moved on to other jobs, but still they will remind me that the things learned with me have been helpful in their newfound work. Also, I have found so much fun in this line of work, as well as having met and talked to many celebrities—opera singers, movie actors, musicians, sports players. And I think there are not many people today who can say they have driven every car, from the Model-T to the 2010 Ferrari. But that's a privilege I have had in my life. Some people today could never drive the cars of the 1950s and '60s, with no power brakes, no power steering, no air conditioning, and no turn-signal lights. Few people today remember how to use hand signals to make turns or stop.

What car do I rate above another? None. Sure, there are powerful cars today of different makes, color, shapes, and speed. But they all can do the same thing; that is, getting you from point A to point B. All cars can let you down anywhere, such as failure to start, flat tires, overheating, or other problems. So I never rate one over the other. In other words, they all have four wheels, steering wheel, gas pedal, brake, and doors. The one difference is the money a person pays for the car.

If you want good, healthy transportation, get yourself a nice bicycle for short trips, not long ones. I used a bike for years because I could not afford a car. I really enjoyed riding my bike. It not was only good exercise, but I could go so many places I couldn't go in a car. Also, I could sight-see up close. I could window shop. I was gas-free and park-free. I would take the bike to the train. I was known by some in my work neighborhood as the bike man, because every time they would see me away from the garage, I would be on a bike.

It's important to be careful when using a bike, certainly on city streets. Drivers cannot see a biker all the time. During my ten or so years of using a bike to and from work, I was almost hit quite a few times. I was thrown from my bike in the middle of traffic a few times. So I picked up good experience on what I could and could not do when riding a bike in the city.

The New Year 1999 was the first time in many years that I would start the year without a mate. I knew I must keep pushing forward, although I was hurting deeply inside. My kids kept me strong. At that time, I was blessed with four grandkids. As of this writing, I have been blessed with fourteen grandkids and two great-grandchildren—enough to keep me busy.

In the latter part of 1999, another death set me back—the death of my youngest brother, Johnnie. Right after he died, I started thinking about another mate to share my life with. I wanted someone with good moral values and a love for Jehovah, because there was no turning back to the life behind after coming so far.

I noticed someone in my congregation who fit that quality. We talked, and I found out that Dolar Marie Branch (called Marie) had a deep love for Jehovah God. She was always present at the meeting and always in the service, talking to others about the things she learned. This was what I was used to; this is what I was looking for in a mate. And Marie had known Mary and all my children; we'd all attended the same congregation together.

The year 2000 came in, and people around the world celebrated as if peace was now upon the earth. People were blinded as to what lay in front of them. As a teacher of the good news of God's kingdom, I found people would not listen to where and how true peace would come upon the earth, as recorded in God's word, the Bible. When 2000 came and went without any major problems, people began to relax. But many people do not understand Satan's tricks. That's exactly what he was hoping—that everyone would look the other way. He knew 2001 was coming and what was coming with it.

In January 2000, I asked Dolar Marie Branch if she would marry me, and she accepted. We talked about a date and set August 12, 2000, as the day. We asked for permission to use the Kingdom Hall, and both of us were very happy when it was approved. While we waited for that day to come, I noted how Marie always kept up with her daily Bible reading, as well as her assignments for the school. Her comments at our meetings were encouraging, and she always had a good social and approachable way about her. All this told me she was indeed a God-fearing person. Now, who now would want a mate who tried hard to live a clean, moral life and who was law-abiding, honest, and an all-around good person?

All my children were happy for me; not even one was in disagreement. They all missed their mother very much, but also they wanted me to be happy as I continued on in my life.

August 12 came, and the weather was just so very lovely. The bridesmaids were dressed in maroon and white. To have Marie's daughter, Romonia, and granddaughter, Tiffany, as part of it certainly made things even better.

Marie's son, Harry, could not be present but also was in agreement and was very happy for his mother and me.

The years 2001 and 2002 were also two great years for working in the ministry with a mate, sharing in Bible study with strangers at their door or out in the street, and then coming home, feeling joy not only from what we were able to teach others but how much they helped us as well. Then in early 2003, Marie's health gave her a setback. But she did not give up, even being bedridden and undergoing a lengthy heart operation. She continued to speak about God's kingdom to her doctors and nurses. When she was discharged, all her home-care attendants were able to learn God's name and his power and wisdom. At the same time, from her hospital bed in the house, she would direct the way she wanted the house cleaned, the clothes washed, and on meeting days, she would dress herself and prepare for the ride to the car in the wheelchair. She kept me going strong.

She would not give in. I could say with all honesty that my life had been blessed bountifully, to have had two mates who loved Jehovah, who had fought to do what was right in a world full of crime and injustice. I mean it when I say they both were spoken about in the Bible at Proverbs 31.

Marie was in a hospital bed with twenty-four-hour oxygen for 112 days. I received so much strength from her; her faith made me strong.

January, February, and March were very mild in terms of weather. My wife, Dolar Marie, was still recuperating from heart surgery and beginning to get some strength back. I was presented with grandchildren to play with. Now I had ten and more to come. This was a blessing, all this love around me. What more could I ask for? All of them attending the Kingdom Hall of Jehovah's Witnesses gave me great joy.

Also, my baby daughter, Caroline, asked me what I thought of her taking on a mate. She had so much respect to ask my opinion. I felt honored. She told me who she had in mind, and I knew him as a fine young man named Daniel, also a servant of Jehovah. Caroline was so happy with my approval. Caroline would fall asleep in death in August 2006, before she could become engaged.

Caroline and I spent a lot of time together, so we got to talk a lot. She told me of some health concerns she had and that she wanted me to pray for her. Sometime I would become so weak when we talked about her health. I knew she was suffering from a dangerous illness, but I wanted to look strong in her presence.

She was under doctor's care and taking tests to help correct the problem. Her sisters and brothers and coworkers were very concerned for her. But although Caroline knew she was ill, she continued to praise Jehovah. She continued to make her meetings at the Kingdom Hall. She really did not burden others with her worry. She was so very sweet to all she would meet. Once I happened to be in the bank where she was a teller. She always told me how happy she would be when I came in the bank. She said I always brought joy to her.

This day I was in the bank at another window and I heard yelling and screaming. I looked over at Caroline's window and saw two people yelling at Caroline. Caroline was so calm, so relaxed, so composed. As always, her lovely smile was on her face. The couple was upset about a banking matter that had nothing to do with Caroline, but they needed to attack someone—anyone; it didn't matter. It just so happened to be Caroline. But Caroline never got upset and returned evil for evil. She just let the bank manager take up the problem.

The couple who was so upset also had parked at the garage I managed. I knew they were nice people. But they never made the connection that the bank teller was my daughter. Later, when I told them the connection, they both were so very sorry. They went back to the bank and asked Caroline to forgive them, which she did. This was the kind of sweet daughter she was, never angry at anyone, always willing to help in any way she could. In fact, that's just what she was doing the day she died.

She had agreed to help out at another bank that was short of staff for the week. I told Caroline that I would drive her to and from work, since I would be on vacation.

We did just that on Monday and Tuesday, and when I drove her home on Tuesday evening, she seemed okay. We made a stop, and she picked up a few things for her house. We drove to her building, and I asked if she could make it up by herself. She assured me she could. The last thing she said to me was "Dad, I love you. Call me tonight." I said, "I love you, too, Caroline. I will call you and pick you up at 8:00 a.m."

When I came home, I forgot to call her and fell asleep. The next morning, Wednesday, I was in front of her building, waiting. I had an odd feeling that something was wrong. Caroline did not come out at the time she should have, and I was worried that she would be late for work. Then I saw her in the window, waving to let me know she was coming down, but she never made it. Someone who lived in the building and knew who I was ran out to my car to tell me my daughter was on the hallway floor. I ran up four flights, and took one look at my lovely daughter and knew she was gone—just that quick from a blood clot in her lung.

The only thing I could do was call out to Jehovah to help me, to please help me stay strong. No parent should ever go through this. It's a hurt that cannot be matched by any other hurt. It doesn't stop. I would wake up hurting and go to sleep hurting. I hurt when I ate, and I hurt when I was doing anything in my life. It never stops. It never stops.

Everything written here has been recaptured from my memory, and I am happy to have shared this part of my life with you. I soon will retire from a life of secular work, but I will never retire from the work of helping others learn about our Grand Creator, **BECAUSE THAT IS THE LIFE I LOVE. I ENJOY THIS WORK AND PRAY TO SET AN EXAMPLE.**

When I lost my daughter Caroline at the tender age of thirty-one, I was hurt deeply and still hurt today. However, knowing the promise that Jehovah holds out for those who are asleep in death—that there will be a resurrection—certainly strengthens my desire to keep moving forward and to learn as much as I can about Jehovah God and his son, Jesus Christ. They are always ready to listen and will respond to my personal needs. There is no other who can give me the support I need to continue to meet the changes of life.

Grand Children	**Great Grand Children**
Chanel	Saniya
Kenny	Tori Jr.
Justin	
Donovan	**Step Grand Children**
Leandria	
Tristan	Mildred
Jordan	Tiffany
Matthew	Whitney
Clark Jr.	Simona
Cameron	Ja'laiya
Englin	
Niah	
Taylor	
Lauryn	
Madison	

June 6th 2005

My Dearest father.

First let me start by saying I Love You. Daddy thank you so much for being such a wonderful and loving part in my life. You are and will always be my #1 man in my life. Each day I thank Jehovah that he blessed me with such a loving and caring father. You have always made things so right. I remember how I loved sitting on the bed next to you and hugging you and talking to you.

Daddy always know that you are muched loved and appreciated in my life. I pray that Jehovah Continue to bless you with good health and a wonderful future. Daddy I Love You, I Love You, I Love You. ☺. Oh I will always be your (noonie) ☺

P.S. Thanks for being my father.

~e else could or would take your place.

Loving You Always
Your Daughter
Carthia Smith

Music Artists I Liked
in the '50s and '60s

Garnett Mims
The Temptations
The Four Tops
Solomon Burke
Marvin Gaye
Percy Sledge
Mary Wells
Joe Tex
Aretha Franklin
Staple Singers
Wilson Pickett
Stevie Wonder
The Beatles
Little Richard
Fats Domino
Elvis Presley
James Brown
Martha and the Vandellas
Hank Ballard and the Midnighters
B. B. King
J. Wilson
Bo Diddley
The Cookies

Country Words and Their Meaning

tote	To carry
yonder	Over there
taters	Potatoes
brush broom	A bunch of dried bushes to sweep yards
tater bed	A mound of dirt and straw to keep yams fresh from the cold
lightwood	A quick-start firewood
switch	A discipline parents used
pump tongue	Needed to draw water through a pump
washboard	Needed to hand-wash clothes
sand spur	A wild thorny bush with tiny spurs
knee baby	A baby just above the baby in the house
tallow	Grease used for cooking or as a healer
slop bucket	Used to feed pigs or hogs
night pot	Used in houses at night for relief
light bread	White sliced bread
drink	Soda
okie dokie	Okay
sweet bread	Cake from scratch

My Thoughts on Discipline

Parents kept a tight control on their kids as they grew up by using a switch. A switch was a long green or dried tree branch. And all kids knew when Mommy picked up the switch that somebody was about to get it.

Another way they disciplined kids was to tell them if they weren't good, the bogeyman would get them. This got their attention because nobody knew who the bogeyman was or what he looked like. They just knew they did not want to meet him.

Yet another way to discipline was telling the falsehood that the Devil would come for them, and take them far down below to his house, and stick a pitchfork in them and put them in the fire. Kids really believed this and would try to be good and obey.

It's sad to say, but child abuse was widespread back then, and the law allowed parents to exact whatever they deemed to be the right punishment to keep their kids in line. And some went overboard. My mother and aunts told us kids about one mother who would heat wire clothes hangers in the open fire and beat her naked kids for such an infraction as bed-wetting. She got caught one day when some tourists who were traveling south got lost and drove into the woman's driveway to ask directions—just as one child ran out the house, screaming. The tourists, not knowing what was going on, demanded to take the child to a hospital. From there, the police came and arrested the mother and sent her away for life.

Home-Grown Medical Treatments We Used When No Doctor Was Close By

*** WARNING, DO NOT TRY THIS AT HOME***

The following treatments were used when I was growing up. I would *not recommend* that anyone try these home-grown treatments today.

Small bushy leaves that grow wild in swamps or at the edge of the woods were used to make tea to treat colds or upset stomach. This worked very well, with no side effects. The country name was catnip tea.

Green pine needles from pine trees were good for treating burning, itching feet. I'd start a small fire in a hole in the ground, place the pine needles over it, and then hold my feet over the smoke for fifteen to twenty minutes—it offered quick relief.

Two spoonfuls of baking soda in a glass of water usually cured the worst case of hiccups. It also was better than most antacids today and cured sour stomachs.

Whenever I cut my foot on a piece of glass—and I cut my feet often—I used the second layer of earth to pack in the cut. The first layer of the earth is always sandy, so I would need to dig a inch or two into the ground to find earth that was more clay-like. Packing this in a cut helped stop the bleeding and quickened the healing. I'd then tie a rag around the foot, and the body's healing system would heal and push out the dirt. I never got an infection from this treatment, but *do not try this today.*

If I stepped on a nail, no problem. I got out the kerosene that was used in our lamps and poured some in a dishpan. Then I'd soak my feet for a while in the kerosene. This would take out the soreness and prevent swelling. After two or three days, I was good to go.

Again, I would not recommend that anyone try this today. It's best to see your doctor.

For tapeworms, Mommy would get out the castor oil. It tasted awful, but two large spoonfuls would send the worms out. How did Mommy know when we kids had worms? She knew the signs. When we were sleeping, we would be on all fours, leaning on both elbows and both knees. Also, we gritted our teeth unnaturally because our stomachs hurt. These were symptoms of a kid with worms.

How did we get worms? By eating half-cooked or raw meat and not moving our bowels each day. Mom would get out the castor oil every Sunday before breakfast. We had two choices: take the castor oil and eat breakfast, or don't take the castor oil and get no breakfast. I always took the first choice.

When there was a newborn baby in the house, the mother would keep two things handy: a fifty-cent piece and a sugar smack. The fifty-cent coin was wrapped in a waistband and placed on the baby's navel to help keep the navel from protruding out. The baby would wear this waistband until the navel healed. This was part of the baby's dress code in the 1950s—every baby used it.

The sugar smack was raw sugar placed in a clean sock or rag that the baby could suck on when the mother wanted to keep it quiet. My mother told me that she made me quite a few sugar smacks. Could that be the reason why I like sugar so much today?

As of this writing, only three siblings remain alive Daisy, Curtis and Lester. All of my aunts and uncles are deceased.

My condolences to the Sparks family. Mrs. Blanche Sparks taught me in first grade. She is mentioned in the beginning of this book. She passed away June 2011 without knowing how much she helped me in my life.

Little Winnie Pooh

Searching 4 You

If I could find the right directions,
I would be there in a matter of seconds,
But you went away and left me no clue.
Baby, baby, what am I to do?

The Greyhound bus, plane, or train,
The speed they have don't mean a thing.
The way I long to see your face,
I would beat Superman in the race.

Now just a call, card, or letter,
But a fax would even be better.
I went AWOL and surfed the Net.
Baby, baby, where are you at?

As I search the highways, byways, through and through,
This endless search is turning me blue.
If you are looking, and I don't see,
Please, please come back to me.

Printed in the United States
by Baker & Taylor Publisher Services